A BOOK OF FACTS

a novel

A BOOK OF FACTS

a novel

Gary Alexander

The New
Atlantian Library

ABSOLUTELY AMAZING eBOOKS

Published by Whiz Bang LLC, 926 Truman Avenue, Key West, Florida 33040, USA.

For information contact:
Publisher@AbsolutelyAmazingEbooks.com

ISBN-13:978-0692438602 (New Atlantian Library, The)
ISBN-10:0692438602

For my favorite ladies: Shari, Tracy,
Michelle and Becky.

A Book of Facts

To make a long story semi-short, on Wednesday 11/17/2010, between 2:45 and 3 a.m., I dreamt that I'd picked up a book in a big-chain bookstore entitled *A Book of Facts: a novel*. It was a best-selling trade paperback in a cardboard dump usually reserved for the dead Swede and all things vampire. *Facts* was arranged alphabetically and chronologically from 1965 to 2012, thus the title. I read the first chapter, flipped over it, and angrily asked Shari, my wife, why the hell I couldn't've thought of it first.

I woke up and realized that I *had* thought of it first. Afraid to go back to sleep and forget it, I stumbled downstairs, caffeinated, and began writing *Facts*. It pretty much wrote itself, the first chapter verbatim from the dream. Over the years, I've fine-tuned it umpteen times.

This is the goofiest thing that's happened to me in all the years I've been in the writing racket. And I truly believe *Facts* is the best thing I've ever written.

Please enjoy.

- Gary Alexander

There is no God. Not yet.

He's spinning His wheels in upper management as Senior Vice President in Charge of Cruelty. When a billion more people die of pestilence, famine, catastrophe, infected dog bites, homicide and war, He'll be eligible for promotion to CEO of the Universe.

— Elmer F. Carter

I know not with what weapons World War III will be fought, but World War IV will be fought with sticks and stones.

— Albert Einstein

APHRODITE, *Venus's only moon, was discovered on October 15, 1965, date of the first public burning of a draft card in protest of the Vietnam War*

The moon was discovered by 19-year-old Jim Wilson, a high school graduate, employee of a slide-rule manufacturer, and amateur astronomer.

On his parents' patio, peering into the telescope he had saved up for from his paper route, Jim Wilson saw for an eyeblink the shadow of a heart-shaped moon on the top of the dense Venusian atmosphere: ♥

He blinked again, but it was gone.

Jim had seen it, though.

He knew he had.

Naming it Aphrodite, for the Greek goddess of love, was an easy choice.

Later asked to explain why he had seen it when professional astronomers in observatories had not, Wilson said that Mercury, Venus and Earth were in a near syzygy, or straight-line planetary alignment. As a comet zipped past, bound for incineration in the sun, solar light ping-ponged from Mercury to the moon to the comet to Venus.

If given the benefit of the doubt on that, he was asked condescendingly by the observatory he immediately telephoned, why hasn't the moon been seen in orbit? Because it doesn't orbit, Wilson explained.

It has to be held in suspension by a gravitational tug of war between the Sun, Venus, and the Earth, he said. Has to be. There was no other logical reason. He was afforded a figurative pat on the head, cheeks bitten at the "logical".

True, some of his explanation was hard science, some supposition. But if they were so smart, let them disprove the latter.

Jim Wilson wrote letters to scores of newspapers and the theatre newsreel companies. All rolled their eyes and ignored him. Who did the deluded kid think he was, young Clyde Tombaugh discovering Pluto in 1930? Clyde was precocious, a professional with good equipment and resources.

A frustrated Jim Wilson wrote to the supermarket tabloids, his last resort. They liked the idea. It was right up their alley, his Aphrodite a staging area for invading aliens. But they dismissed the story as being too complex for their core readership.

The full crush of those disappointments came later, but on Saturday, October 23, 1965, after receiving his paycheck, a still-euphoric Jim Wilson took Laura Jones, his 20-year-old girlfriend, out for a burger and fries.

In those days, to have a girl friend older than oneself was scandalous, but neither cared. Nor did they lose sleep that he was a middle-class boy whose parents adored her and she was a rich girl whose parents despised him. She was the only person on Earth who believed in his discovery of the moon Aphrodite and would be for years.

They drove to their favorite parking place, a wide spot on a potholed fishing road. It was a clear, balmy night in an Indian summer, so when they climbed into the back seat, they kept the top down on Jim's parents' 1962 Chevrolet Impala SS.

One thing led to another. And another. Jim tried to prolong their lovemaking by thinking of other things. Non-erotic things like the specifications of the Impala, which they had rocking on its springs.

Specifications Jim knew by heart: *Body by Fisher, Ermine white color, 3560 pounds, 209.6 inches total length, 283 CID overhead-valve V-8, 275 pound- feet torque, one 2-barrel carburetor, $3026 factory price, 11-inch expanding-drum braking system —*

It didn't work.

Simultaneously, they lost their virginity and handed a rabbit a death sentence.

Jim Wilson and Laura Jones snuggled on cool Naugahyde, her dress up, his pants down, a patina of perspiration, blood and semen bonding them.

They listened to crickets and glanced at the full moon.

Besides the joy of the coupling itself, Laura took further pleasure in knowing if Father Sir knew, he'd have a cow. Her Mumsy too, if she was sober when she got the news and remembered it.

Jim was in the midst of a living dream.

It was the best evening of their lives and always would be.

ARMAGEDDON X7. Weapon *system developed in the mid-1960s by the Jones Armament and Research Company. Armageddon X7 was designed to employ concentrated radio waves that penetrated the thickest jungle to contact the enemy hiding within. The waves targeted and destroyed eardrums, and other soft membranes.*

Per a confidential Jones memo, "The enemy's brains will cook like porridge, causing an agonizing death. A revolutionary gem of a weapon."

On Thursday, November 25, 1965, Roscoe Snails, Vice-President and Senior Liaison Officer (i.e. chief lobbyist and bagman) of Jones Armament and Research reported to Robert Jones, President and CEO. That the day was Thanksgiving Day was irrelevant. If Mr. Jones worked on a holiday, and he usually did, senior management did too.

Snails sat across from Jones and told him that they had a tentative deal.

Jones's eyes bored through him. *Tentative?*

With goose bumps under his pinstripes, Snails reminded his boss that Armageddon X7 was by far their most complex project and it was still on the drawing board.

Jones reminded Snails that Jones Armament always delivered. The magnesium grenades that were guaranteed to kill, killed. The mines the size of marbles, scattered along the Ho Chi Minh Trail, gave the little slimeballs a humdinger of a hot foot.

And the successful electromagnetic trials we've done, positive stepping stones to the X7? Christ Almighty,

Roscoe, can we move along? How many more dogs and cats do we have to dispatch in the name of science?

Roscoe Snails was eager to be out of there. With what passed for a smile, he said he did have encouraging news. The people he dealt with close to the people LBJ pushed around said that the President was rumored to be very enthusiastic about Armageddon X7.

To paraphrase the President of the United States of America: If they won't listen to reason and stay on their side of the 17th Parallel, the only way to get the little fuckers out of our hair is to kill 'em. Get the Jones boy and his machine cracking.

Sir, we essentially have a blank check, Snails added. All we are required to do initially is to show progress.

Bob Jones rubbed thumb and forefinger together.

Yes sir. Plans, Proposals, Payoffs.

Bob Jones winked. The Three Ps, Roscoe. All paper. Get on with it, first thing in the morning.

Roscoe Snails, his number two man, hurried out the door. The remainder of the bootlicking lemmings followed, shutting off lights as they went.

Bob Jones sat there, enjoying the semi-darkness and the solitude.

Enjoying it doubly because he wasn't home for Thanksgiving. The cook and household staff would have a lavish feast prepared. Gwen would've directed it, pacing around and getting in everyone's way, never without a whiskey sour in her hand. By now, she'll be sound asleep in one of their six bedrooms and the staff would be fidgeting, waiting for company that hadn't been invited.

Bob Jones' idea of entertaining was a business lunch

or cocktails at the club. He couldn't risk an at-home function with Gwen there. Gwen who was usually not there when she was there. Regardless, Bob Jones had no friends, only underlings and clients.

He liked it that way.

The closest facsimile to a friend was Roscoe Snails. Roscoe was a tiny man who had hair slicked back like Defense Secretary Robert S. McNamara's and gray eyes that revealed nothing. He was creepy, yeah, but he'd lie across railroad tracks if Bob Jones ordered him to.

Laura, their only child, had a standing invitation for Turkey Day and any other day. Fat chance. She was a true rebel without a cause, a pretty girl who took every opportunity to spit in his face, blaming him for her Mumsy's boozing and who knows what else.

A college dropout, Laura had attended business school and went on to work a flunky job as a computer keypunch operator. If computers interested her, he'd said the last time they talked, Jones Armament and Research had one of the monstrosities in the basement. The power usage for it and the computer room's air conditioning cost a bundle.

Better yet, she could come aboard as a management trainee even though she was a girl. They'd be breaking new ground.

No thank you, Father Sir.

The worst slap in his face was her choice of boyfriend, a pencil-neck with glasses who stared idiotically into his cheap telescope at the night sky.

The Wilson kid, a loser who worked at a nothing job assembling slide rules. The rest of his résumé — paperboy and in high school part-time pinsetter in a bowling alley.

Wilson was clearly headed to the top, a world-beater.

Hell, if she was turned on by oddballs, Jones Armament had its share in the computer room. They wore wrinkled clothes, were clumsy, had bad haircuts, smudged glasses, and big asses.

Mr. Right awaited her four floors down.

One consolation about Laura's Jim Wilson was that if he had a dick, he wouldn't know what to do with it.

AZZTOUND 2111D. *In 1965, it was the most powerful and advanced computer in the world. The 2111D's magnetic drums had 6MB of random access memory and each of its tape drives held 256KB of core memory. Features included vacuum-equipped feed arms, card readers, 36-bit integers, main processor logic, and floating point arithmetic.*

On November 29, the Monday after Thanksgiving, Laura Jones sat at her keypunch desk, feeling queasy. She wondered if it was morning sickness or if she was coming down with a bug. She had missed her period three weeks earlier.

She'd broken the news to Jim after Thanksgiving dinner at his home, where he lived with his folks, David Wilson Senior and Brenda Wilson, and Jim's 10-year-old twin brothers, David Junior and Richard. Mr. and Mrs. Wilson were lovely people who adored each other. David Junior and Richard were quiet, well-behaved boys.

Mr. Wilson worked as a body and fender repairman and Mrs. Wilson was a housewife. Their rambler in a middle-class suburb had two bedrooms, one bath, and a carport. The backyard was fenced. It had a swing set that would be coming down soon, when the twins got a little older. The family planted a vegetable garden every spring.

Jim shared one bedroom with the twins, who slept on the opposite wall in bunk beds. Accustomed to a mansion and luxurious furnishings, Laura thought the home should be impossibly cramped, but there seemed to be more than enough space.

Father Sir once said that "the dump could fit in his billiards room."

Fuck him.

Laura was learning to swear without blushing. She'd have to try it out on Father Sir the next time she saw him, see what color *his* face turned.

Fuck you, Father Sir, you piece of shit. Kiss my ass. Father Fucking Sir.

Cursing in her head seemed so natural. The words had a cadence.

Like nursery rhymes for adults.

The savory smells of Mrs. Wilson's fantastic cooking went with them into the Wilsons' 1962 Impala SS. They drove to their parking place. Into the back seat they went, this time with the engine and heater on, and the convertible top up.

They made love, their faces against each other's clothing, on which the aromas of roast turkey and stuffing and sweet potatoes and aftershave and perfume lingered.

That was when Laura told Jim, saying that she needed to find a doctor soon and hoped her company's health insurance paid for it.

He said that if they were married, there should be no problem. She asked if that was a proposal. If it was, he shouldn't feel like she was forcing him into marriage.

And she shouldn't think he was diving into marriage to avoid the draft or to do the right thing, he said. They were exempting married guys with kids. For now they were.

Jim fumbled in his pants pocket, a good trick since they were wadded below his knees. He gave her a small velvety box. He'd been carrying it around, saying he hadn't decided how to propose. He'd been too chicken to.

Laura opened the box and squealed.

Jim placed it on her finger and kissed her hand. He said she'd need a magnifying glass to see the diamond.

She told him not to be silly. She told him she loved him.

He said he loved her too and was that a *yes*?

Yes yes yes yes yes yes yes.

When? each wondered aloud.

Yesterday, she wished.

Last week, he wished.

He said he couldn't picture her dad giving away the bride. Oh, Father Sir would like to give me away all right!

But not to me.

No, not to you, you naughty boy. Any man with character and without money isn't good enough for his little girl.

There were wedding chapels right across the state line and no waiting period.

You've done your homework, man of my dreams.

He bet that Mom and Dad and the twins would love to take next Friday off and go over there with us. We'd get it done Saturday.

Your dad could give me away.

He'd love to!

Their honeymoon would be quick and cheap, she suggested. They'd overlook a waterfall near the chapel for an hour or so, and then head back to their room.

Ten minutes at the waterfall and back to the room, he said.

She playfully slapped his bare butt and said, someday, when they can afford it, they'd have a real honeymoon, at the closest motel to the big observatory that'd been renamed The James Wilson Planetarium, after he got his just due for discovering Aphrodite.

He told her that she was a perpetual honeymoon. She said to please slip under her; we'll find out if we can do it here with her on top. Keep tonight's honeymoon going.

Now, typing punch cards, Laura counted the minutes until Saturday, December 4, 1965. They had called ahead to a chapel and made an appointment for noon. Her lunch here was at noon. It was 11:27 now, so it'd be — let's see — 7233 minutes until they were man and wife.

Laura Jones hadn't gone far in high school math, not past plane geometry, but she had a gift for numbers.

She liked numbers.

Numbers spoke to her.

Numbers sang and danced inside her skull, awake and asleep.

Numbers were playthings, like: $3^2 + 4^2 = 5^2$ or $9 + 16 = 25$.

Like: $5^2 + 12^2 = 13^2$ or $25 + 144 = 169$.

She paused to flex her fingers, looking through the glass doors of the garage-sized room that housed the AZZTOUND 2111D. She watched lights blink and tape reels spin. She listened to whirring and clicking and clacking inside the air-conditioned inner sanctum, envying the programmers at the controls.

She worked in one row with five other keypunch ladies. There were six more behind her in a second row. Laura spent more time staring at that machine than the other 11 combined. She couldn't get enough of it.

It was like seeing her favorite sci-fi movie over and over again.

B

BA'U, was *a remote atoll in the South Pacific, an oval slab of coral the size of San Diego. It was the epicenter of an earthquake measuring 7.9 on the Richter scale. Ba'u crumbled into the ocean as if a micro-Atlantis. The quake occurred at 1:05 a.m. local time on Saturday, January 1, 1966. Tidal waves were expected to threaten neighboring atolls and islands. Tsunamis may reach the South American coast.*

Gwen Carter Jones awakened on New Year's Day with a hangover. The head-splitter wasn't a result of too much New Year's Eve celebrating and bubbly. Gwen hadn't celebrated anything and she woke up with a hangover every day. All 365 or 366 of them, January 1 to December 31, were interchangeable.

Gwen Jones sat on the edge of the bed, head in hands. After a couple of deep breaths, she reached to the nightstand for her cigarettes. Gwen was in her mid-forties, trim and naturally blonde. She was still an attractive woman, but those days were numbered. The facial creases of a chain-smoker were beginning and gin blossoms had sprouted prematurely.

Beside her cigarette package was a Christmas card that had been torn in half. On it was the Star of Bethlehem or some other star of religious significance. Gwen tried to remember what they had done on Christmas Day.

Probably nothing. Bob was surely at the office and she'd given Daisy Allen and the staff the day off after they'd prepared her pitchers of whiskey sours and a plate of cold cuts.

Beyond that, who could say?

Gwen opened the card pieces. With trembling hands, she placed them side by side.

She flattened them on the nightstand and read:

Dear Mother and Father,

I'm sorry I mailed this to you late. I did because I was afraid to ever send it to you. I was afraid of your reaction. My husband Jim talked me into it. Yes, Jim Wilson and I are married. We tied the knot on December 4. We didn't tell you or invite you, knowing how you feel about Jim.

We're going to have a baby, but it wasn't a shotgun wedding. We love each other very much and we thought you had the right to know that you're going to be grandparents.

Love,

Laura

Gwen slumped back to the edge of the bed. Bob despised Jim Wilson, but Gwen didn't. He was a nice young man. Gwen remembered that and not much else when Laura brought him by, whenever that last was.

Obviously, her daughter, who was carrying her grandchild, was ashamed of her. Her and her bad habits and her perpetual stupor.

She doesn't deserve to be that baby's grandmother! She is a disgrace!

Avoiding mirrors, Gwen Jones squeezed and twisted

the cigarette package, and flung it into the garbage, and put on her robe. Before she went into the dining room, she laid the object of Bob's anger in the nightstand drawer, making a mental note to tape the pieces.

Daisy Allen, granddaughter of a slave, was waiting at the edge of the kitchen, saying good morning, ma'am, how are you. The way she habitually did, even though she knew how Gwen was and that it was no longer morning.

Gwen said good morning in return.

She noticed the morning newspaper on the dining table. She hadn't read a paper in ages. Bob always took it the office to study the business page and check the stock market listings. Since it was a holiday and he'd presumably stormed out in anger, the paper was hers. She looked at the front-page headlines. There was a major earthquake in the South Pacific and the American troop count in South Vietnam at the end of 1965 was 184,300.

A weekly news magazine they subscribed to was also on the table. Gwen paged through the magazine. It seemed as if every other page was an advertisement for cigarettes or hard liquor. At least those were the pages that caught her eye.

Daisy said that she sent the rest of the staff home and hoped Mrs. Jones wouldn't mind, as they'd been in early to get all their chores done. Mrs. Jones said that she'd done right.

Daisy seemed relieved. She told Mrs. Jones that her pitchers of whisky sours were prepared and would she like her usual toast made? Mrs. Jones said no thank you. Please pour the whisky sours down the drain, brew a large pot of strong coffee, and make me a big breakfast of bacon, scrambled eggs, and the toast. Then you go on home to your family too. She could take care of herself. Honestly, she could. She'd have her breakfast in the living room as always.

Yes ma'am, Daisy said, trying to hide her surprise, reminding Mrs. Jones that it was a weekend as well as a holiday, so her soap operas weren't on. It's football all day long, she said, rolling her eyes. Lordy, her husband's in seventh heaven with all those bowl games, five or six of them.

Football, Gwen Jones thought. She hadn't watched a game in ages. Bob didn't watch TV or go out to movies either.

Could Daisy recommend a bowl game?

Well, no ma'am, she couldn't, but her husband talked and talked about the Rose Bowl. UCLA and Michigan State were playing and starting soon. Daisy hadn't the foggiest why it was such a big deal, but it was.

The Rose Bowl it is, Gwen said.

She took the newspaper into the living room and turned on the television. It was a 25-inch color set, the best money could buy. While the TV warmed up, she found the channel number in the paper.

When the picture came fully on, Gwen turned the dial to the Rose Bowl's channel. Her timing was perfect. The referee and the team captains were doing the coin toss. Gwen sat down to read the paper, eat a nice breakfast, drink coffee, and watch football.

So different was her day, she could have materialized in a parallel universe.

It was going to be a splendid day.

Yes it was.

BREAD. *A feed-the-needy charity formed by Gwen Carter Jones on Monday, January 10, 1966. (Note: This nine-day gap will be clarified 795 words later.)*

She immediately recruited Mary Ann Snails and other wives of Jones Armament and Research Company's top officers.

She passed the hat, and they volunteered their time and money without complaint. In Jones Armament's distaff hierarchy, Gwen Jones was president and CEO.

The transformation of Gwen from alcoholic zombie was a miracle. The volunteers couldn't believe their eyes and ears. Unlike her tyrannical prick of a husband, Gwen was a sweet person. They'd do anything for her

Their initial funding financed 2000 square feet of warehouse rental, a 1964 Ford Econoline van to pick up donations from supermarkets and food distributors, and advertising. The price was right on the space. It was not in a swanky neighborhood. Its present tenants were rats and tomcat-sized dust kittens.

Asked if BREAD was an acronym, Gwen's answer was no. Bread, the lack thereof, was an age-old symbol for hunger.

BREAD came to her out of the blue, so BREAD it was, she said.

Thanks to the clarity of sobriety, she didn't say.

Bob Jones hadn't the slightest idea how Gwen snapped out of her daze and threw herself into this wacko welfare program of hers. But it kept her out the hell of his way. The one time they spoke of it, he referred to their intended recipients as "loafers and spades and moochers".

Gwen Carter Jones joyously committed herself to working 60-hour weeks at her warehouse office and behind the wheel of the van. So soon after Gwen's cure, without alcohol, she had hour upon hour to fill, useful hours as opposed to useless hours.

Now, why this charity, any charity for Gwen, one might ask?

Priority number one was filling time. Doing so ASAP, lest she backslide. Soap operas and whiskey sours had wasted so much time. Time that was finite. Time that could not be recovered and respent.

She ruled out seeking gainful employment. Gwen didn't need the money and she was almost 42-years-old, out of the job market too long to find anything that wasn't menial.

Gwen Carter had married in 1944 at age 20 at the height of World War Two. She was swept off her feet by a handsome, dynamic 22-year-old businessman who owned a successful recycling business, finding and selling scarce metals vital to the war effort. His office and yard were across the street from the furniture wholesaler at which she typed invoices and bills of lading.

There had been whispers that her groom's business practices were not aboveboard and that he had purchased his draft deferment.

Gwen ignored the rumors. Malicious, unfounded and envious gossip, they were.

Bob Jones worked long hours and was gone a lot, and soon became distracted when he was home, bordering on cold. To shunt womanizing from her mind, Gwen rationalized his coolness on the pressures he faced.

Nonetheless, philandering did stick in the back of her mind. Fearing a rocky, unstable marriage, without consulting Bob, she was fitted with a diaphragm, making Laura an only child.

Twenty-some years later, she believed that if he had had affairs, they were infrequent. Her husband had no interest in any human being other than himself, and the wealth and power he acquired.

Bob Jones, who was a too-convenient excuse for Gwen Carter Jones's boozing.

However, on Saturday February 7, 1966, Gwen was not at BREAD, completing a 60-hour workweek. She was at Jim and Laura Wilson's $65/month one-bedroom apartment.

The Wilsons had chosen it as their first marital home not only for the price, but for its location above a small neighborhood bakery and its wonderfully airborne sugar and yeast that wafted upward.

The spiders came at no extra charge. They decided that they could tolerate spiders until the baby was born. If they couldn't get rid of them or the landlord wouldn't, they'd move on. They'd have to anyway. There wasn't enough room in the crackerbox for three.

Gwen Carter Jones was at their apartment because there'd be no baby. Six days ago, when the bleeding began, Jim and Laura went to the nearest emergency room. Laura miscarried in the lobby.

Gwen had been sleeping on the couch and planned to do so as long as she was welcome and useful. She was with Laura in the bedroom during her waking hours and doing what else was required of her. Jim was at work. Gwen knew that the Wilsons wouldn't take a dime from her, so she didn't insult them by offering.

What they did take from her was reconciliation with her daughter. They accepted it from a sober, smoke-free mother-in-law/Mumsy. Mumsy who was now who she'd been during Laura's childhood: Mommy. Mommy no longer looked like Mumsy, nor behaved like Mumsy. Her cheeks were a healthy pink, not blotchy red, and her eyes were alive, as if by magic.

How did this magic come to be?

Why and how was Mumsy now Mommy?

Magic pills and the magic of love made it come to be.

On the fateful New Year's Day five weeks ago, a worried Daisy Allen returned to check on her missus at the start of the Rose Bowl's fourth quarter. According to her husband it was a dandy of a ball game in which UCLA was upsetting highly-favored Michigan State.

Earlier in the day, Daisy busied herself with housework in a futile attempt to keep her mind off Mrs. Jones. She didn't care that UCLA was upsetting highly-favored Michigan State.

Mrs. Jones didn't care about the upset in the making. She was by then fidgety and trembling. Going cold turkey on two addictions was harder than impossible.

Upon arrival, Daisy helped Mrs. Jones up from the living room sofa, undressed her, gave her a pill, and got her into bed.

Thanks to the pill, Mrs. Jones slept 15 straight hours. Daisy was there for her when she awakened, with homemade chicken noodle soup and whole wheat toast and another pill. This regimen lasted three days.

When Mrs. Jones tried to get out of bed, Daisy steadied her as she regained her feet. Mrs. Jones didn't ask what the pills were and Daisy didn't say. She loved her mistress and would do what she had to do to get her through this living hell.

Whatever those pills were, Gwen had lost her nicotine craving, but she would for every day of her life want a drink.

Mommy Gwen was back in the bedroom after getting Laura to eat chicken and dumplings. She stroked her forehead to help her get to sleep, as she had when Laura was a small child. Looking at her as she did, she was thinking that mother and daughter could be twins separated by 19 years. Same slimness and small features. They were pretty, but not cheerleader pretty.

Laura demanded and got frequent hugs and kisses from her Mommy for her tears and cursing. Her daughter's swear words were new to Gwen's ears, albeit understandable in the circumstances.

The emergency room doctor had told Gwen and Jim that temporary depression after a miscarriage was normal. He couldn't say why she miscarried. One common cause was genetic. Jim and Gwen didn't want to hear that.

Both came from small families. Gwen had lost contact with her only sibling, a brother, Glen Carter, who then lived in a different time zone.

Left unsaid was that this might've been the Wilsons's one and only chance. Further left unsaid was the hysterectomy that might by necessity be ahead for Laura.

Dave and Brenda Wilson spent what time they could at the kids' apartment. Dave took a day off at the auto body shop and Brenda brought hot meals, including pot roast, a favorite of Laura's.

The Wilson's identical twins, David Junior (so named by virtue of being 14 minutes older) and Richard, accompanied their parents one time with homemade get-well cards.

When Gwen was out, Bob came by too, probably timing it that way. It was a perfunctory visit. Laura remembered little of it except Father Sir repeatedly glancing at his gold Rolex.

Even in her despair, Laura felt comforted, for she had a family: Jim, Mommy, her in-laws, and brothers-in-law. Mommy, from whom she had extracted a promise — crossing her heart and hope to die, swearing on a stack of Bibles to never ever to touch a drop again, grandchild or no grandchild.

BYRNES, JACK. *Jack went to be with the Lord on Saturday, March 4, 1967, when he succumbed to natural causes. He was the beloved son of the late Adrian and Helen Byrnes. Born on June 16, 1927, Mr. Byrnes received a BS in mechanical engineering and an MS in mathematics. He was employed as a senior project engineer at the Jones Armament and Research Company. Services are pending at the Sequinson Funeral Home*

Private Jim Wilson couldn't attend Jack Byrnes's funeral even if he knew the man and wanted to bid him farewell. Jim had been in United States Army Basic Combat Training since mid-February 1967. Not a college boy and no longer an expectant dad, his draft status reverted to 1-A.

The Selective Service System scooped him up in a hurry. With an American presence of 386,000 troops and climbing fast, and over 7,000 dead GIs and five times as many wounded to date, the War had a growing requirement for warm bodies.

At the induction center, as Jim and other inductees awaited the results of their physical exams, all they could talk about was what they hoped was wrong with them. None of the draft bait was eager for heart disease or cancer, mind you, but they yearned for whatever they can live with and the Army can't.

Nearsightedness, farsightedness, trick knees, high blood pressure, low blood pressure, flat feet, slipped disks, neuritis, neuralgia, post nasal drip, hair growth in unusual places, the heartbreak of psoriasis.

They prayed for a reverse Lourdes, where 4-F was the miracle.

Jim Wilson was not optimistic. If you had a pulse and could fog a mirror, you were in. And in he was, inside his basic training barracks, standing at the position of attention in front of his bunk, shivering.

They'd been ordered to keep their windows wide open all night because there'd been cases of spinal meningitis on the Post. He wondered how risking pneumonia and hypothermia fended off meningitis.

This was Army logic.

Which defied logic.

Jim and the rest of his platoon were housed in wooden World War Two barracks, with two rows of side-by-side bunks. Each man had a wall locker and foot locker. They shared a latrine with a rectangle of open commodes. Of all the indignities a buck private endured, Jim thought that communal shitting was the worst.

All for the princely monthly salary of $87.90. Plus room and board — three hots and a cot, as was the slang.

Jim Wilson had two more weeks of Basic. Then he'd be off to AIT (Advanced Individual Training). Jim guesstimated that eight of the 10 fellow draftees in his platoon would study to become an 11B10, also known as 11Bravo10 or 11BangBang10, the MOS (Military Occupational Specialty) for Light Weapons Infantryman. Following graduation from the Army's notion of grad school and two weeks leave, off to South Vietnam it would indeed be.

During his boozy going-away party at home, a friend of Jim Wilson's who'd been in, stationed in West Germany, told Jim to tell anybody who cared to listen that he knew how to type.

He didn't know how to type. Hadn't touched a typewriter key in his life.

Tell them anyway. Any swinging dick can carry a rifle.

Lying by a mere eight fingers, Jim informed the personnel sergeant who made MOS assignments that he was a full ten-finger typist capable of 30 words per minute. Thanks to the fib and high intelligence test scores, he was assigned to clerk typist school.

Jim Wilson was not naïve. Vietnam outfits required clerks too, to in-process troops.

And to out-process those going home, vertically and horizontally.

Waiting for the inspection team, Jim thought of Laura's last letter. Parts of it were hard to read because of all the lipstick kisses. In the newsy part of the letter, she wrote him about Jack Byrnes's death, saying that she thought she might have met Byrnes when she was a kid. Father Sir might have had him over for dinner.

Her Mommy had heard two rumors concerning Jones Armament:

The Government Accounting Office (GAO) might audit them. Reason unknown.

An employee was killed by an accident on a top-secret project.

Next, she mentioned in passing, in one sentence, that the bleeding started again and she had to have a hysterectomy, and please please please, don't worry, she's fine. In the pink.

Jim had gone behind the barracks, out of sight, and cried into his sleeve, to hide tears and to muffle sobs. One could receive an early discharge for being a sissy, but it'd be a less than honorable discharge.

God, Jim missed his Laura, his beloved wife! She was as brave as any medal winner.

In came the barracks inspectors: their platoon sergeant; the company's first sergeant; and the brand-new company commander, a freshly-promoted first lieutenant not much older than Jim. The CO brought with him from another company a reputation for being chickenshit.

The lieutenant came in with a swagger. That shiny new silver bar on his cap, you'd think it was four stars.

He was living up to his chickenshit rep by dropping a quarter on bunks to see if it bounced or not on the tightened blankets. If your blanket flunked, you flunked, regardless how shiny your boots and brass were, and how perfectly arranged your belongings were in the lockers.

Maintaining the position of attention, Private Jim Wilson did not give a diddly damn if the asshole's quarter bounced on his bunk or not.

How were they gonna punish him, ship him off to Vietnam?

Heels locked and eyes ahead, he daydreamed of Laura.

He fantasized of a post-Basic MOS as an astronomer.

Of doing two years of service to his country hunting for Aphrodite.

Hunting for validation.

≈≈≈

Jim Wilson was on Laura Wilson's mind day and night, night and day. The numbers that did vaudeville acts in her head were moved offstage in favor of her husband.

This weekend as she worked 16-hour shifts, thoughts of Jim still held sway over her complex, exhausting duties.

Laura had been promoted from keypunch operator to programmer assistant trainee, and as such was on the crew that had a Monday morning deadline to get AZZTOUND 2111D through the glass doors and into a semi-truck, and AZZTOUND 3111E in its place, up and running, completely programmed, ready to power up, making lights flicker in a five-block radius.

The new version was half the size and twice as powerful as the old. The engineers boasted that it weighed less than a Cadillac.

Amazing, she thought, as she helped steady a hand truck as a beefy colleague rolled out a tape drive. Simply amazing technology.

A creation of Buck Rogers and Albert Einstein.

C

CARTER'S GAP. *By means known only to himself, Elmer Free Carter predicted natural disasters by what he termed a Gap. Mr. Carter defined a Gap as a period in which nobody died, nobody anywhere in the world.*

To maintain a metaphysical balance between life and death, a natural or unnatural disaster must follow.

Of course, the Gap was short, often infinitesimal. The latest Gap, the one that landed him in jail again, by Elmer Carter's calculation, lasted a fraction of an eyeblink, an instant of an instant, roughly 1/5000 of a second.

Elmer's daughter, Gwen Carter Jones, learned of his latest Gap brouhaha on Tuesday, July 4, 1967, when her father called from the city jail.

He told Gwen it was the same old goddamn thing – police brutality, the goddamn storm troopers we pay taxes for, denying an American citizen his First Amendment right to free speech.

Meaning he'd been handing out his mimeographed warnings on a street corner. As aggressively as the religious cults and their pamphlets.

Where and when, Dad?

Where and when what? The disaster?

You know what I mean, Dad. Your leaflets.

Oh. Yesterday afternoon. On the corner of Third and Main.

Great. The center of downtown, on the day before a holiday, people leaving work early, anxious to get to their cars and busses.

Elmer Carter said it wasn't his fault. Some joker shoved him hard when all he did was try to save his life. Defending himself, Elmer retaliated with a poke in the nose and received a poke in return. Who the hell wouldn't? The guy could've shoved him out in traffic in front of a bus.

Right, Dad, it's never your fault. She'd be there soon and hung up on him.

Gwen had been setting up for a Fourth of July barbecue, with the able assistance of Laura and Jim, who was home on leave from clerk typist school prior to assignment in Vietnam. Bob was at the office, so she was led to believe. Ever since Jack Byrnes's mysterious death, he'd been staying away at night more times than not.

Jim's rank had increased from Private E1 to Private E2, so he was drawing $100.00 per month, plus $50 hazardous duty pay when he arrived in Vietnam.

Rolling in dough, Jim joked, the Wilsons felt obligated to bring side dishes of potato salad and coleslaw. Daisy Allen was there too as a guest, under strict orders to not lift a finger.

Gwen Carter Jones excused herself, went to the jail, paid the bail, and collected her scrawny, intense father. Dad had been a bit tetched since retirement three years earlier. A chemist for food and beverage companies, he had too much time on his hands in a big lonely house and no way to scratch a scientific itch.

To contribute, to save lives, as Elmer Free Carter put it.

He believed that the food additives and preservatives his team developed did save lives. Yeah, they had unpronounceable names and were also used in the rocket fuel that got the astronauts into orbit.

But your food didn't spoil, did it?

His vernacular had become gamy as had been his personal hygiene at times. Gap was his cause, his obsession. If his little girl thought it was screwball, well, that was her problem.

On the way home, Gwen couldn't hold it in as she had before, humoring him, babying him, trying to talk some sense into him.

She told her dad that the Gap nonsense absolutely had to stop!

The desk sergeant had said that they'd shrugged off the previous incidents because of his age and harmless eccentricities, but their patience was at an end.

No more slaps on the wrist. He was lucky the party he smacked didn't press charges.

And that wasn't all, she shouted as he interrupted her. Somebody is going to get hurt. You'll land in the hospital. If it's the other person, *you'll* land in prison.

Her dad tapped a red spot on his schnoz and said somebody *did* get hurt. All he'd tried to do is tell the rancid son of a bitch to batten down the hatches, to prepare for the worst. Ma Nature, the sadistic old broad, she was gonna blast away with one of her disasters and it could take a bead on his neck of the woods.

Out there performing a public service and look at the gratitude he got. If you're at the wrong place at the wrong time, Gwen, you can bend over and kiss your ass goodbye.

Furthermore, these people out there, your average citizen, they have no respect for science. Goddamn Luddites, half of them probably believe the earth's flat.

There's *always* a disaster somewhere, Dad.

Elmer conceded missing that department store fire over there in Brussels, Belgium last month that killed 300-plus, but you can't catch them all. His timing nailed that Ba'u earthquake and tidal wave right on the nose, didn't it? The one that killed 9000 people in those islands where they used to have cannibals?

Gwen gave up and changed the subject, saying that she was bringing him home for a barbecue – ribs and chicken and potato salad and cold beer, his favorites. He said that was swell and had he ever told her how foul grub was in the slammer?

Yes, he had.

They got a new special, this mystery gravy that has the consistency of quicksand. They ladle it on top of –

Then stay out of jail, Dad!

Elmer Carter looked over at his little girl. Bless her heart, she was a reformed drunk and a sweetheart. His beloved Hazel had been gone since Gwen was 20 and newly married to that slicky boy.

They'd cut off one of Hazel's tits, then they had to cut off the second. Too late. The cancer had spread like the plague and it was all over in two painful months.

His son, Glen, the goddamn worthless bastard and draft dodger and sneak thief, he'd been gone to parts unknown for years. Still around, mooching off them when Hazel died, he hadn't even bothered to come to his own mother's funeral. Said he worked late and had slept in.

Blamed it on the alarm clock. The "working late" was guano too. Elmer could count on his fingers the number of days the boy was able to hold down a job.

Speaking of shitheels, he thought. Where's that goddamn robber baron of a husband I told you you shouldn't've married, he asked?

Elsewhere, she said.

Good. He wouldn't trust him as far as he can throw him. He'd try, though, if it was off the top of a skyscraper.

Yes, Dad.

Jimmy, who knocked up my granddaughter, he's not a bad kid. It'll be nice to see him before they load him on a troop ship.

They fly them now.

Elmer told her (for the zillionth time) that he was ripe meat for the military between the world wars, too young for the First, too old for the Second. That police action or whatever it was in Korea, too old for that too.

This thing Jimmy has to fight in, he said, he didn't understand what those little Orientals were doing to get us so riled up and this domino theory they have back there in Washington, DC.

Killing Krauts and Japs, that was one thing, but he wasn't even sure where this South Vietnam country was on the map.

Germans and Japanese, Dad.

Yeah, yeah. That's now. Then they were Krauts and Jerries and Nips and Japs.

Gwen shook her head at the stubborn old man and said she hadn't known where Vietnam was either.

And Jim was a clerk typist, not a rifleman.

He asked if she had the morning paper at home.

She did. Why?

To start keeping an eye out for a hurricane or earthquake or volcano eruption or airliner crash. Mark his words, a biggie was right around the corner.

CESIUM ANOMALY. *Cesium is a highly-reactive metal, one of few metals that is in liquid form at room temperature. Cesium ignites spontaneously when exposed to air, so it must be handled or applied while contained in an inert gas such as argon.*

However, in the development of ARMAGEDDON X7, something went very wrong. A component in the cluster of magnetrons and high-voltage vacuum tubes in the death ray's intensification assembly should not have exploded. But it did.

The cesium coating inside a sealed part ignited in its argon atmosphere, killing a technician by the name of Eric Hayes

Three days later, Jack Byrnes, the senior project engineer in charge of designing the magnetrons and high-voltage vacuum tubes, went home for lunch and didn't come back.

On Tuesday October 31, 1967, in his penthouse bed, Bob Jones relived that inconvenient occurrence as he ofttimes did. Last March fourth, he'd been summoned from his office suite because of a mishap. He'd heard what he thought was a car backfiring.

It wasn't.

He hurried downstairs to see a god-awful mess, the wreckage of ARMAGEDDON X7 and a dead employee. One had to use care not to step on shattered metal and glass.

Not to mention blood and flesh. The employee, whoever he was, looked as if he'd been clawed by a tiger.

Bob Jones closed his eyes and clenched his fists. Jones Armament and Research had never suffered such a tragedy.

Months and months of work gone in a split second!

The police and an ambulance were called. Everybody went through the motions. Mr. Robert Jones, the company's president and CEO, was an excellent actor when he had to be.

Sniffling and wiping his eyes, Jones told the police officers how distraught he was over the loss of life of a valued employee, dear friend, and wonderful human being. He promised to pay funeral expenses and compensate Mr. Hayes's family, to take care of their needs indefinitely.

Like Jack Byrnes, Jones was informed by the personnel department that his "dear friend" Eric Hayes had no family.

In a sense he didn't. Jack's people were dead. Eric's had disowned him.

Turns out Hayes was a fairy. Roscoe Snails, bagman par excellence, paid the deceased's roommate to keep his mouth shut and to stay away from a burial without a service (also paid for by Jones Armament).

It was vital that the cause of the employee's death be hushed up.

Nor would it do any good if it got out that Jones Armament and Research had a faggot on the payroll. A security risk vulnerable to blackmail was a no-no.

Roscoe Snails was behind the idea of spreading the rumor that due to undisclosed family problems unrelated to work, Eric Hayes committed suicide by eating the barrel of a .38 Special in the men's room.

The scuttlebutt that Jack Byrnes's cause of death had

been due to "natural causes" was also Roscoe's doing. An undiagnosed enlarged heart that called it quits on him at the tender age of 39.

Not the true story.

A grief-stricken, overwhelmed-with-guilt Jack Byrnes committed suicide by going home for lunch and swallowing the barrel of a .38 Special.

Bob Jones knew that to the U.S. Government suicide in the midst of a vital project was not the best of all worlds. It was a calculated risk.

The Government Accountability Office (GAO) might begin breathing down his neck because of delays and cost overruns on X7. For the moment, though, the GAO had bigger fish to fry, but Jones was careful how deeply he reached into Uncle Sam's cookie jar.

Throttle back, Bob Jones told himself. Take it slow and easy. Think low profile. Think long-term.

Roscoe was told by his lobbyist connections that LBJ had casually wondered out loud to his staff how that invention that'd fry those pesky Vietcong was coming along. They were multiplying like rabbits. Them and the North Vietnamese who weren't minding their own fucking business.

They said, yes sir, Mr. President, they'd look into it right away. Underlings reporting to the presidential staff did try to check, but Roscoe Snails and his lobbyist counterparts headed them off at the pass. Roscoe and his boss had faith in their lobbyists. They believed that an *honest* lobbyist was an oxymoron.

President Johnson forgot about the X7 too. With close to half a million troops in Vietnam and anti-war protests at home, he had other things on his mind.

Like people wearing WHERE IS LEE HARVEY OSWALD WHEN WE REALLY NEED HIM? buttons on their shirts.

Trick or treat, Lyndon, Bob Jones thought as he rolled off of Mary Ann Snails. Mary Ann, who would do things in bed that his dried-out prude of a wife would not. The wife who probably thought he was a womanizer.

He wasn't. But when he needed poontang, he *craved* it.

Mary Ann was in his penthouse suite for sex too, a service her husband hadn't provided lately, which was fine with her. She did not want a "relationship" with Bob any more than he wanted one with her.

He was a fairly decent piece of ass, though, on the scale of one to ten, a seven.

After sex, Bob Jones wanted silence, to be left alone afterwards until he first spoke.

Fine with Mary Ann. What did they have to talk about?

Odd gal, Bob thought as she lit a cigarette. He didn't smoke. His body was a temple, thanks to vanity and time at a gym. He was no Rock Hudson, but he had all his hair, a strong cleft chin, and a flat belly. When you first met him, you got a solid handshake and demeanor that said *I won't live forever, but you'll beat me to hell.*

Very odd gal, sitting up in bed, knees up, legs apart, she was an aspiring hippie. Christ, he knew she was zeroing in on 40, old enough to be the mother of most of those long-haired, dope-smoking freaks out on the streets with their flower power and draft card burning and any other un-American activities their addled pea-brains dreamt up.

Her long hair growing longer, Mary Ann wore tie-dyed this and that, jangly jewelry. Armpit and leg hair was unshaven, that actually kind of a turn-on. She was shapely and dark, French-looking back when she was normal, now evolving into a gypsy.

Mary Ann was Gwen's number two at that BREAD thing, supervising other Jones Armament wives who squandered their time volunteering, rather than keeping house and cooking like respectable housewives and mothers.

BREAD's soup lines feeding the lazy, the bums and the jigaboos.

It was beyond him.

For the first time, after banging her for weeks, he asked if she thought Gwen was on to them, the little woman aware that some of Bob's long hours were not spent at his desk.

Mary Ann didn't think so. He'd neglected to ask her if she felt guilty cheating on her best friend. It was outside of his sensitivity, Bob Jones being Bob Jones.

Did she feel guilty? That was a tough question, but the answer was probably no. Now that Gwen saw Bob through the clearer lens of sobriety, she told Mary Ann how very much she loathed him. Therefore, they were man and wife strictly on paper, as she and Roscoe were.

Sexually, it was open season.

Mary Ann did wish Gwen would step out on the slime, though. It'd help Mary Ann through the twinges of guilt that came and went.

The hippies she admired opened Mary Ann's eyes, had opened up a new world. Free love, dope, et cetera — simple pleasures she'd missed being Roscoe's little wifey.

Mary Ann Snails asked Bob Jones if he gave a flying fuck if Gwen knew. Or was he just making conversation.

Her filthy mouth was another turn-on. Bob smiled.

Observing that he was aroused, Mary Ann crooked a finger. Bob Jones obeyed her command.

≈≈≈

In or out of bed with Mary Ann Snails, Bob Jones had not given his pencil-necked loser of a son-in-law a thought for some time.

Home or overseas, on this Halloween or any other day, Private First Class Jim Wilson had not given his piece-of-shit father-in-law a thought for some time.

Every day was Halloween for PFC Jim Wilson, a Halloween where every home gave the trick-or-treaters popcorn balls containing razor blades.

PFC Wilson's duty station was an infantry company in South Vietnam's Central Highlands, between Pleiku and Ban Me Thuot, three kilometers from the closest village.

The plus for the Highlands was a milder climate, far less oppressive than Saigon's steam bath.

The minus was their isolation.

At night, the only sounds were what the Vietcong wanted them to hear.

The company's mission was to accompany the South Vietnamese Army (ARVN) in an effort to interdict the Vietcong. The company was under orders to go where the ARVN led them, and the ARVN did their damndest to avoid the VC.

The enemy chose where and when to make contact.

PFC Wilson was his company's clerk. He worked at a desk in a tent that served as the orderly room. He was relatively safe compared to the 11BangBangs, the grunts. Most were good guys, draftees from the 50 states. They passed along interesting lore that was in no geography book.

One from Fairbanks said that you knew it was -50° or below if you spit and it froze before it hit the ground, bouncing like a marble.

Another from Anniston, Alabama told of restrooms in bus stations for Men, Women and Colored, and drinking fountains for Whites and Colored.

PFC Wilson typed morning reports that depressed him morning, noon and night. As he'd guessed, his morning reports recorded new troops that processed in and those who processed out for home, The Land of The Big PX.

Too many of the out-processings in rubber body bags.

PFC Wilson was likable, albeit an oddball, a dud with his head in the clouds. At night, he looked into the sky when there were no clouds. If asked what he was looking at, he'd point out Venus and the Milky Way and the Andromeda Galaxy.

He did not mention Aphrodite.

If anyone disliked him, they had the good sense to hold their dislike within. Nobody fucked with a company clerk.

If a company clerk was in a retaliatory humor, he'd change the coding on his morning report, an honest mistake that'd give one grief. By delaying a promotion or removing a dependent or in any number of viciously subtle ways.

PFC Wilson typed for the commanding officer, executive officer, and first sergeant too, his superiors with whom he shared the orderly-room tent.

He typed for some of the grunts as a favor, guys who could barely read or write. You didn't have to be a Rhodes Scholar to serve in the United States Army as an 11BangBang.

He typed for himself. He wrote two or three letters a day to Laura, even when there was nothing to say. He wrote to his folks and his kid brothers. He wrote to planetariums and major universities, relentlessly selling his discovery of Aphrodite.

His family wrote back.

The planetariums and universities did not.

PFC Wilson wrote with ten-fingered fury on his Underwood portable. He'd finished first in clerk-typist school, with the highest typing speed in his class.

Jim typed so loudly and fast, making such a vibrating racket on the flimsy desk, he didn't hear the first *whoomph.*

The orderly room was vacant. The CO, XO and first sergeant were at noon chow (Armyese for lunch), unavailable to alert him.

The *whoomph* was a round discharging from an American-made 81-millimeter mortar. A mortar was a steel tube that sat on the ground, steadied by adjustable steel legs.

To fire a mortar, a shell was dropped into the tube. The projectile fell onto a firing pin that ignited the cartridge primer.

Whoomph.

Up it went.

The round weighed approximately seven pounds including stabilizing fins. This particular weapon had either been stolen by the VC or sold to them by a South Vietnamese ally. If one knew what one was doing, and the VC surely did, the weapon was accurate up to 3000 yards.

Veteran troops who had been in Korea knew what the *whoomph* was.

Incoming, they yelled.

Incoming!

Upon impact, the American-made 81-millimeter round exploded, discharging and disbursing cast-iron shrapnel.

After the third *whoomph,* Jim Wilson heard yelling and explosions in the direction of the mess tent, the primary target.

The fourth *whoomph* was the last he heard.

Three days later, Laura Wilson received a telegram from the Department of Defense.

CUTS GALORE. *Exactly what it says.*

This was a breakdown of Jim Wilson's injuries from the mortar attack, courtesy of Victor Charles:

Lost: his left eye and two fingers on his right hand.

Gained: 512 stitches from cuts, approximately 90% of the shrapnel removed.

A blood vessel nicked too. A fast Medevac to a field hospital saved PFC Wilson's life

Rehab was slow, physically and emotionally. Army doctors said that controlling infection as it spread from wound to wound was like trying to eradicate fleas in a kennel. There was a limit to how much penicillin they could pump into Jim. After an onset of diarrhea and a rash on the inside of his mouth, they reduced the dosage.

Emotional recovery was slower.

Jim Wilson roller-coastered from upbeat to downbeat to upbeat to downbeat.

Upbeat because 27 men died in the attack and he'd been spared.

Downbeat because of his maiming.

Upbeat because he was home, spoiled by Laura and her loving care.

Downbeat because of the guilt of being alive when 27 men in his outfit were not.

Among them were the outfit's CO, XO and first shirt.

While he, a clerk-typist, not an 11BangBang, was minding the store and typing.

When he wasn't upbeat, he pretended he was, so not to drag his wife down with him any more than he already had.

You looked through a telescope with one eye, not two.

The second was irrelevant.

Jim opted for an eye patch instead of a glass eye. He didn't wear the patch to project a swashbuckling image, like a half-assed pirate, or as a lead-in to telling war stories.

The thought of having to remove the glass eye to clean it as if dentures repulsed him.

That and one eye going in a direction, the other staying put.

Laura and Jim knew that he'd have to cease moping and find a job and return to normalcy.

The slide rule company had welcomed him back.

His company's linear slide rule, or in the slang a slipstick, was made largely by hand of traditional materials – hard woods, steel ends, and a glass or clear plastic cursor. Engraved characters on the plastic veneers were ultra-precise. His company's slipsticks performed basic math calculations as well as logarithmic and trigonometric problems.

Laura Wilson loved to play number games on her slipstick.

Laura, who hadn't gone beyond plane geometry.

Laura who taught herself long division in the second grade for the fun of it.

Laura who had kept *that* accomplishment to herself since she was a little girl.

He couldn't do the precision work with eight fingers and eyestrain due to a single eye. They promised to find a job for Jim elsewhere in the organization. A pity job, he knew.

His own battle with self-pity was struggle enough. The

last thing he wanted was sympathy from fellow employees while he did busywork.

Laura encouraged him, saying it was a stable company and that he'd have a future there. Privately, she felt otherwise. Learning on the job as a programmer assistant trainee, learning fast, she had been promoted to programmer. The computers she programmed continued to shrink in size and swell in power.

Someday computers will render slide rules obsolete, she thought in awe. For an affordable price, you'll be able to buy a machine for your personal use. It'll be no larger than the portable dishwasher they had in their new home and movable on casters too.

Lift the lid to access a keyboard and a small screen.

Do slide-rule math on it and much much more.

Even balance your checkbook!

College for Jim was an option they hadn't discussed because of money. Wouldn't it be wonderful if they could afford it, him majoring in astronomy? It was something to think about.

Their new home was a three bedroom-one bath rambler in a suburb 20 miles from downtown. Laura's promotion and Jim's disability pension had made the down payment possible. The back yard was large and fenced, with room to romp for the child they couldn't have.

How many times had Laura looked out at it and conjured a swing set and a tire swing in one of the two trees? She'd lost count.

The Wilsons settled in by mid-May and sent out invitations for a Memorial Day housewarming and barbecue.

Everyone responded to their RSVP and showed for Laura's and Jim's Monday May 27, 1968 function:

The Bob Jones and Roscoe Snails couples, who due to various antics were odd couples.

Dave and Brenda Wilson and their 12-year-old twin sons, David Junior and Richard.

Elmer Carter.

Attire was eclectic:

Mary Ann Benson Snails, braless inside a sleeveless tie-dyed blouse, the cuckolded Roscoe wearing a blue suit, white shirt, no tie.

Brenda Wilson in a well-worn flowered dress, Dave's white socks topped by dark slacks.

Their boys in matching T-shirts and shorts, most of the time off to a side playing catch with a tennis ball.

Unnaturally quiet and well-behaved little boys, good students excelling in math and science, Jim thought. He'd been no hell raiser when he was their age, but their deportment was oddly proper.

Bob Jones in the confectionary colors of a golfer, though far pricier than anything sold at a pro shop. Gwen Carter Jones stylish in pink shorts and white blouse.

Jim Wilson in a Beach Boys uniform of chinos and madras shirt.

Laura Wilson's hair in a beehive hairdo, complemented by mauve cotton slacks and a white top.

Elmer Carter in an ensemble that'd been slept in and was indefinable.

At the sight of Jim, the guests tried to be nonchalant while exchanging handshakes with an eight-fingered man who had an eye patch and multiple scars on his face and arms. Only sociopathic Bob Jones succeeded.

Elmer Carter, never at a loss for inappropriate words, in an effort to lighten things with levity, asked Jim if he was smooching a porcupine.

Polite, forced smiles all around, except Gwen who wanted to strangle her father, and Jim, who startled everyone including himself by laughing out loud. In a weird way, he was enjoying the attention.

Any attention was preferable to being called a baby killer. That happened twice in town, on the sidewalk. Jim's injuries were a dead giveaway.

He'd been asked if he received them in Vietnam.

Reading their attitudes, he said he had, and what was it to them?

The first came from a long-haired young guy, tieless in a paisley shirt and corduroy suit. Jim was too stunned to react. Laura was with him and did react, screaming in the guy's face, showering the creep with every commonly-known four-letter word and some that weren't.

Jim smiled whenever he thought of it, how the freak shrunk inside his paisley.

The second came from a demented-looking young woman with curls hanging to her shoulders and a peace-sign necklace. She screamed in his face, showering him with every war-crime cliché short of calling him Adolf Hitler.

Jim slapped her face so hard his hand stung.

The woman and her companions were too stunned to react.

Jim smiled whenever he thought of it.

Jim grilled chicken and ribs on the barbecue. Laura

had side dishes at the ready – potato salad, green salad, and rolls. Cold soda and beer were in good supply. A dessert of Laura's brownies capped the meal.

Small talk was smaller than small. Socially, the couples were oil and water. Bob Jones said nary a word to his son-in-law, who reciprocated.

Bob and Mary Ann sat at opposite corners of the picnic table, so there'd be no temptation by her to play footsie.

They need not have worried. Gwen didn't care enough to be curious or jealous.

Who knew what Roscoe thought, even Roscoe?

The corporate bagman ate daintily, eyes on his food, cutting up his meat with knife and fork, the only person who didn't eat with their hands, red sauce smeared on their faces.

Bob's fascination with his gold Rolex embarrassed Gwen, who was the first to say, well, they should be running along. Tomorrow was a workday, and they had a big shipment of donated canned food coming in at BREAD.

People filed out after thanking and complimenting the host and hostess.

Elmer Carter was the last to go. Until his daughter retrieved him, he stared into the blue sky. When his daughter had him by a hand, he'd said, no sweat, there hadn't been a Gap lately, so there was no lightning or hail or tornado on the horizon.

Jim cleaned up outside as Laura loaded the dishwasher.

Laura started it and dried her hands, looking out the

kitchen window.

Grampa had stood on the exact spot where Laura Wilson's imaginary swing set was. Out of nowhere, *adoption* popped into her head.

Can she talk Jim into it?

Can she talk *herself* into it?

DACHAU HOAX. *On Thursday July 24, 1969, there was a bizarre story on page two of the front section of the morning paper. A man who called himself Reichsführer Adrian Newt, commander of* The White Christian Minutemen, *held a press conference.*

The purpose of the conference was to state that the Apollo 11 moon landing was a hoax, a fraud. What we saw on July 20 was shot in a studio. It was a hoax just like Dachau and the other so-called German concentration camps were, all arranged to demonize the greatest leader in the history of mankind, Adolf Hitler.

Asked why the moon landing was a hoax, Newt said that the money set aside for Apollo 11 was transferred into Wall Street banks and the Jews who ran them, and then percentages siphoned into the pockets of government officials who made the conspiracy possible.

Jim Wilson shook his head as he read the story and looked at the photo. On a hanging banner behind Newt was *The White Christian Minuteman* symbol, Jesus Christ crucified on a rough-cut wooden swastika, not a cross. As if he was to be drawn and quartered.

Jim was an agnostic, but found this *too* creepy.

Newt himself was creepy. Chubby, receding chin, small round glasses, wispy mustache, old-timey haircut with shaved sidewalls. His eyes were beady and heartless.

Jim pictured him loitering around schoolyards with his fly unzipped. He looked kind of familiar, an old Nazi named Him- or His-something. Jim paged through the GREE-HORT book in a set of encyclopedias his folks had handed down to them.

There he was, Heinrich Himmler, supreme commander of the SS, the Gestapo, and the death camps, arguably the worst mass murderer in history. Himmler died a quarter century earlier. Assuming they weren't related, Newt was doing his utmost to be the fiend's doppelgänger.

Jim Wilson put down the newspaper. Otherwise, he'd be thinking about Newt and have nightmares. He hadn't gotten to the paper until late afternoon. It was almost time to start out for BREAD, where he worked swing shift for minimum wage as a warehouse picker.

His mother-in-law's charity was going great guns, feeding lots of hungry people. Jim's job was boring and low-paying, but satisfying. He had accepted Gwen's and Mary Ann's offer because it wasn't charity, it was at a charity.

They had rented adjacent warehouse space, raising their square footage to 5000 square feet. BREAD had a second van too, a beater but it was free, a donation, as was the labor to get it into reliable running condition.

Laura was at work. She rode in with a neighbor, a secretary who worked in the same building. The neighbor operated Laura's company's new word-processing machine, so they had plenty to talk about. The word processor was in a separate room and required two weeks of training.

Laura had two programmers under her now and sometimes stayed late. If they were lucky, they saw each other for ten minutes per day. Their schedules made the weekends all the better, on the Impala's backseat or not.

Jim's telescope stood in the corner of the dining room. Most paper boys spent their earnings quickly or saved for a camera or a bike. Every penny of Jim's had gone toward the $199.95 price of his telescope, a small fortune.

Before leaving, he looked at it again. The skies were clear and starry after sundown. Jupiter was unusually close to Earth. Last night after coming home, Jim had taken his scope to the patio and focused on the giant planet.

He saw its bands. He saw its fabled red spot, a storm that had lasted hundreds of years, its diameter larger than Earth's.

Also Jupiter's four largest moons: Io, Europa, Ganymede, and Callisto. Known as the Galilean moons, they were first seen by Galileo Galilei in the 17th Century. Jim saw them as fiery pinpricks, like miniature stars.

Of course, he'd aim at Venus too.

Aim at the area on the planet's surface that he'd seen Aphrodite.

Jim Wilson opened the garage door and got into the hand-me-down 1962 Chevy Impala SS convertible. He started it, thinking of the back seat and the magical nights on it with Laura, especially the first.

After a few drinks one night, they recreated the magic in the garage on the Naugahyde seat. Now they did regularly (not that they didn't in bed too), with or without a few drinks.

Bed was nice, but not the same as the Impala. Not quite.

Jim backed out, thinking of adoption. They had decided to go ahead, to adopt a Vietnamese orphan. There were many of them, far too many.

The procedure, though, was daunting. The interviews, the red tape, the scrutiny. The money. They'd have to apply for a bank loan.

It'd happen.

They knew it'd happen.

They'd make it happen.

It was just a question of when.

≈≈≈

Bob Jones hadn't read the morning newspaper and no way was he going to read the afternoon paper. He knew what the front-page headline and lead story was going to be: JONES ARMAMENT AND RESEARCH ACCUSED OF FALSIFYING DATA ON SECRET DEATH RAY.

His people had solved the cesium-coating problem on ARMAGEDDON X7 and completed a working prototype.

Top-level officers of Jones Armament went to the pound for animals, to "give them a loving home". Most were slated for the needle anyway, so why not?

The first firing made at a fenced and guarded compound 10 miles from Jones Armament was encouraging. At 100 yards, a 27-pound mongrel's brain cooked into a steaming mound of goo, smoke curling from its ears.

Executives and technicians alike yelled and cheered and jumped up and down and spoke of uncorking champagne.

The dog's name was Spike.

Then trouble.

At 200 yards, a 14-pound, short-haired orange tabby jumped as if kicked and hissed at the business end of the death ray.

His name was Randy.

At 300 yards, the lethal radio waves had no discernible effect on Rover, a dog, and Kitty, a cat.

Rover barked and Kitty meowed, impatient to be cut loose.

Examination of the 200-yard target area revealed scores of dead fleas. Randy, the cat, sat, yawned, and licked its privates as Bob Jones and his team stood dumfounded.

At Spike's demise, Bob Jones had yelled and cheered and jumped up and down too. Now he was sitting up in his penthouse bed as the summer sun descended, painting neighboring buildings a pinkish-orange. He was thinking that for ARMAGEDDON X7 to be effective, the Vietcong had to come to it, 100 yards or closer. He doubted that they were so inclined.

Years of work and tens of millions of taxpayer dollars later, Jones Armament had developed the world's most expensive alternative to flea powder.

With Roscoe Snails' able assistance they should have been able to keep a lid on the fiasco and hold the Pentagon at bay. But there'd been a stool pigeon from within who gave or sold the bad news to the press. Jones Armament had 250 on the payroll and nobody was talking.

Jones' best guess was a disgruntled employee on the shop floor, perhaps a fudge-packing buddy of the homo killed in the explosion. An employee, holding a grudge, who had been biding his or her time before getting even.

Mary Ann Snails was not smoking a cigarette after their sex. She rolled marijuana in cigarette paper and lit up. She'd evolved into a full-blown hippie, smoking pot and participating in anti-war demonstrations. The whole nine yards, Bob Jones thought in disgust.

He took the joint from her and had a "toke" as the parasites called it. The drug didn't make his problems go away, but it leavened them in the short-term.

Out of the corner of his eye, he saw her staring at him, an irritating habit of late. If she was fishing for pillow talk, she was out of luck.

Bob didn't love or particularly like Mary Ann, but he was *addicted* to her.

Mary Ann enjoyed Bob's irritation. She knew how he felt about her. She didn't take it personally. Bob Jones didn't like anyone but himself.

She had been staring at him because he was a near-perfect specimen of manhood: Looks, brains, nice body, high achiever, financially successful.

He was still an okay piece of ass, although even colder and more remote each time they got it on.

On a scale of one to ten: five-point-five.

Mary Ann was nine years younger than her husband. Nevertheless, she was deeply into her thirties when the maternal instinct kicked in. It blindsided her, catching her totally by surprise, and could not be suppressed.

Roscoe and she had tried in the past, mostly her idea. Roscoe, who had the sperm count of a eunuch.

Without looking at her, Bob handed the joint back to

Mary Ann. He was *really* uptight about something. If she asked, he wouldn't tell her. But she didn't ask because she didn't care.

Cognizant of the risk her age posed, menopause a mere decade down the road, she had flushed her birth control pills down the toilet. This near-perfect specimen of a sperm donor was going to be uptight and then some if his tadpoles hooked on. He'd go berserk when he received the happy news.

But Bob Jones had genes that should be passed along once more and she was the right girl for the job.

DOUBLE BOUNCE. *On April 24, 1970, after a four-month journey, a Soviet probe attempted to land on Venus. If all went well, it'd transmit telemetry for up to an hour before being roasted and crushed to death.*

The Venusian atmosphere was primarily carbon dioxide. CO2 trapped heat so well that surface temperatures ran as high as 900°. *Venus was toastier than Mercury. Venus' atmospheric pressure was up to 100 times higher than Earth's. A mild breeze would flatten an Earthly metropolis.*

This probe had a mind of its own. It did not enter the atmosphere from a programmed orbit and descend into the harsh medium. It bounced along the top of it twice, as if a flat rock skipped across a pond, then off to the sun to be vaporized, but not before transmitting a few minutes of telemetry.

Unlike some other Soviet failures in the exploration of Venus, this one was kept hush-hush by order of the scientist in charge of the project.

He had his reasons.

He was thinking of the future.

The future too for his top two assistant scientists who saw what he saw. Providing they obeyed his orders and kept hush-hush.

Under his breath the chief scientist muttered, Leonid Brezhnev, you with the bushy eyebrows, our leader with no brain, you whore of the capitalist running dogs, go straight to hell. Why cannot we have Josef Stalin back to lead us? Hail to Uncle Joe!

The chief scientist and his two top assistants nicknamed the probe c□aчo□ or "BOUNCE".

Mary Ann Benson Snails gave birth to a seven pound-four ounce boy she named Ocean Robert Benson. Ocean had not been born with three arms and one lung, as his natural father warned (see bottom of page).

He was the most beautiful and perfect baby in the whole wide world.

Gwen Carter Jones was present in the waiting room. Daisy Allen was present. The Wilson clan was present, including Jim and Laura Wilson's newly-adopted two-year-old daughter, Quyen.

The baby boy's biological father was not present in the waiting room. When Mary Ann Benson Snails began showing, Bob Jones expressed mild curiosity, bluntly asking if she shouldn't go on a diet.

Mary Ann announced to Mr. Sensitive that she had good news. He was going to be a proud papa.

His response was a string of shouted obscenities. In summary, he told her to dress, get out of the suite, and don't come back. He told her to break the good news to the real father if she could narrow him down from the free love hippie scum she had one-night stands with and gangbanged.

Mary Ann blew him a kiss from the door, then flipped him the bird with a smile.

Purple-face enraged, he told her that if there was *good* news, it'd be that he got lucky and didn't catch VD from her. And if the diseased bastard she was carrying wasn't born with three arms and one lung.

Roscoe Snails was not present in the waiting room. He had not been present at the Snails residence for months.

Either Roscoe didn't know Mary Ann was carrying his

boss's child or he didn't care. Following the ARMADEDDON X7 scandal instigated by an employee/traitor who leaked the weapon's failure, Jones Armament and Research lost credibility and contracts. Employment plummeted from 250 to 62.

Among the 75% gone was Roscoe Snails. He hadn't been laid off. He went voluntarily, prior to the newspaper story, citing a job offer through one of his lobbyist cronies.

Bob Jones asked about the job.

Roscoe was vague, saying only that it was with an organization with connections to the government, a covert organization. He thanked Bob for the years of employment, but he was too intrigued by the opportunity to decline it.

Roscoe went home, immediately packed, and moved out. His wife didn't ask why and where, and he didn't tell her. She was wearing a maternity blouse then, a solid clue she was with child, but Mary Ann was invisible to Roscoe. When he went out the door with his last suitcase, Mr. and Mrs. Snails didn't even say goodbye.

Other loved ones in the waiting room were eager to see mother and child. With the exception of Quyen Wilson. She was asleep on her daddy's lap, making it a twofer of happy moments, one behind the delivery room door and the second, this breakthrough in father-daughter intimacy.

At the South Vietnamese orphanage where Quyen had lived until adoption, they had done the best they could, but there were too many children and too little food.

The Wilsons were perplexed when little Quyen cried her eyes out when they took her food bowl away even though they knew she was full. More disturbing, she became tense and rigid at any physical contact by her parents.

The adoption agency explained that this behavior was perfectly normal. Their daughter was unaccustomed to unlimited food and intimacy.

Give it time, they said.

Jim and Laura smiled at each other, their eyes moist.

Giving It Time was starting to pay off.

DUBIOUS. *The word that best described Roscoe Snails' feeling regarding the order he had been given. "Dubious" ran through his head for the umpteenth time on the night of Saturday June 10, 1972 as he led his team to the 6th floor of the Watergate Hotel and Office Building. Four men, Roscoe and three others, made their way to the headquarters of the Democratic National Committee.*

They picked the lock and entered easily. Carrying flashlights, under his direction, Roscoe's men examined the contents of desks and filing cabinets.

Roscoe Snails' chain of command was clandestine and layered. This burglary order and other work he performed came from someone who had been given orders by someone who had been given orders by someone else. Roscoe Snails didn't know where the orders originated and didn't want to know.

He had a checklist and a top-of-the-line, built-by-hand, 35-millimeter Leica M5 rangefinder camera. The Leica's 50-millimeter Summilux f/1.4 lens was so fast that pictures could be shot in a closet without a flash.

Speed-reading documents as his underlings turned pages, Roscoe was poised to photograph those pertinent. After 45 minutes, they'd gone through everything. He had checked off nothing, photographed nothing. It would've been a waste of film.

They straightened up the offices and went out of the DNC and the building. What a futile waste of time, he thought. They could have been caught and arrested for nothing.

Roscoe wouldn't be here risking his freedom and his life if not for his slatternly wife and Bob Jones. He would have remained at a prospering Jones Armament, stonewalling X7's failure.

Their liaison wasn't the point. He couldn't care less that they were having an affair. He cared even less that Jones sired an illegitimate child by her. What irked him was that they believed they were pulling the wool over his eyes. Obscenely coupled between the sheets, laughing at him.

And later, not caring if he knew, Mary Ann flaunting her pregnancy.

Roscoe Snails could not endure ridicule, he could not endure condescension. That was why he made anonymous phone calls to select members of the press, muckraking bulldogs who lived for rocks to peek under.

A risky night of futility at the Watergate, he thought again, a week and two days later. A small news story buried in the local section of the paper made Roscoe laugh, this a man who seldom smiled.

Five knuckleheads had been arrested the previous Saturday, June 17, 1972 inside the DNC.

Had they been searching for what he had searched for?

On that day, oblivious to any event but the future catastrophe of which he sought to alert —the populace, Elmer Carter, stood at a downtown street corner with his mimeographed Gap warnings of impending disasters.

To trick the police, he'd moved two blocks from his usual Third and Main Street venue to Second and Central.

Police officers were close by, a greater than average presence.

They had no interest in the cuckoo well known to

them— Elmer Free Carter.

Elmer was in a mellow mood. Smiling and saying hello to passersby, graciously giving his Gap warning to those who chose to accept one, was as aggressive as he got.

As a come-on, he drew an arc on the sidewalk with chalk. If somebody asked, he'd ask if the individual saw it as concave or convex.

Why?

Easy. They'd pause so he could offer them a handout.

Clever, but Elmer had no takers to his bait. That was hunky-dory today. He was looking forward to a birthday party in a couple of hours.

He was mellow, that is, until four men approached. The pair on the outside were burly. They looked like bouncers for a topless bar. The one in their middle was average-sized. The fourth, who trailed, was average too.

The one in the middle of the goons looked familiar. Despite blue skies, the threesome wore full-length raincoats.

Aha!

Elmer Carter escaped service in the world wars, but he had studied the conflicts in detail. He knew the major players. One was that Nazi death camp boss, a pal of Hitler's. And here the son of a bitch was, an escaped war criminal walking by, not 10 feet from him.

The ferret-faced louse.

Elmer didn't question why the man looked the same as he had 30 years ago. For all he knew, Dr. Josef Mengele, the Angel of Death, had concocted a magic potion for him.

Elmer Carter threw aside his Gap warnings and charged Heinrich Himmler, the escaped war criminal.

Reichsführer Adrian Newt and his bodyguards were bound for the city plaza, where they planned to stage a surprise rally of *The White Christian Minutemen*, to rail against the International Jewish Conspiracy and the repeal of slavery. One of Newt's escorts was his brother and second-in-command, Oberst (German for colonel) Skip Newt. The Oberst brought up the rear, the story of his pathetic life.

Others under his command were to rendezvous there, one with a bullhorn. In service to the white Christian race, Newt planned to speak until he was arrested, giving him and his righteous cause invaluable exposure from the newspapers and TV news.

But Newt would not be the one under arrest. Elmer lunged and grabbed the back of his raincoat, shouting *goddamn war criminal citizen's arrest goddamn war criminal citizen's arrest.*

Elmer slipped, tearing the raincoat away as he fell, exposing Newt's SS uniform. The soft, weak Reichsführer slipped too, striking the back of his head on the pavement, pummeling the warped brain within.

Newt's *Minutemen* thugs and his brother Skip jumped Elmer, who swung wildly, biting and kicking, going for the nuts.

He booted Skip Newt squarely in the crotch, lifting him on his toes, dropping him in agony.

Elmer put up one helluva good fight before being taken down. Men and women observing the melee came to the aid of the old man.

The police department had been tipped off to Newt and his rally. The nearby officers who'd had no interest in

Elmer Carter did now.

They separated the participants, as if referees pulling apart a football pileup after chasing a loose ball. Three of the five principals in the skirmish were taken to jail: the storm troopers and Elmer Carter.

The fourth, an unconscious Adrian Newt was taken to a hospital.

Intracranial bleeding had worsened en route.

Adrian Newt was pronounced dead on arrival.

Official cause of death: Bilateral pulmonary thromboemboli.

Cause of death in plain English: Complications from falling down and breaking his crown.

The fifth, Skip Newt, was taken to another hospital, where a crushed testicle was amputated. His left calf and ankle were badly scraped and cut from the impact to the pavement.

Newt had no medical insurance. He told them to put a dressing on it and do nothing more.

Big mistake.

≈≈≈

As Quyen Wilson blew out four candles on her birthday cake, Gwen Carter checked her watch, certain that she'd given her father the time of the party. She was worried. Dad was scatterbrained, but he adored Quyen.

By Jim's and Laura's calculation, June 10 was their daughter's birthday ± five days. Neither the orphanage nor the adoption agency could estimate it any closer, such was the chaos in 1968 South Vietnam.

Quyen Wilson spoke good English and she was beginning to read. An extremely bright girl, her speech was above average for a four-year-old. She did continue to be standoffish to her parents and other adults.

With two-year-old Ocean Carter, it was a different matter. The youngsters had clicked. There was no other way to put it.

The two-year difference in their ages (772 days ± five days, per Laura Wilson's mental calculation), made them an honorary big sister-little brother pair, sans sibling rivalries.

Their relationship went further than that in an indefinable way.

The partiers polished off the cake and ice cream. The kids played on the swing set in the back yard of the Wilsons' three-bedroom suburban rambler. The swing set Laura visualized when *adoption* first popped into her head.

Quyen and Ocean were polite to each other, took turns, and didn't fight. They chattered endlessly to each other, Quyen studiously talking down to his level. Any annoyance on her part was expressed by her speaking to him in loud Vietnamese.

Everybody watched them, entranced, as if spectators at a sporting event.

Proud grandparents of Quyen, Dave and Brenda Wilson, and their 17-year-old twins, David Junior and Richard.

Former hippie/pot smoker, Mary Ann Benson and Gwen Carter had reclaimed their maiden names as surnames and were housemates now with young Ocean.

Gwen was happy to have them in the big lonely house while she fought her estranged husband for it.

The Wilson phone rang. Laura answered it and waved to Gwen. She went in, guessing who it was and where he was calling from.

Gwen was right, but she did not excuse herself to bail him out.

Trembling, she hung up the phone.

Elmer F. Carter was being held without bail.

E

E PLURIBUS UNUM. *Latin for "out of one, many". It is a motto on the Seal of the United States, as adopted by an Act of Congress in 1782. E pluribus Unum has 13 letters, representing the 13 original colonies. The back of the $1 dollar bill includes E PLURIBUS UNUM on its Seal of the United States.*

Waiting in a gas line, Gwen Carter's stomach was in knots.

Knots no Boy Scout could tie or untie.

She shouldn't have let her car get down to fumes, but she had much on her mind.

Thanks to the Arab oil embargo and her distractions, there she sat in line, six cars ahead of her, everybody eager to fill their tanks with gasoline the station had jacked up to an outrageous 42.9¢ per gallon, the bandits.

When this station had put up a green flag, motorists congregated as if drawn into a black hole.

Please, don't replace it with your red flag until seven more cars filled up.

The red flag that was code for no-more-gas-in-*our*-tanks.

Sitting tensely, idling, she was thinking that a whiskey sour would taste *so* good. A nice dark cocktail lounge. A cigarette in her fingers too. Gwen had those thoughts when under stress.

How long had it been?

Going on eight years.

Hang it there, girl!

Wednesday October 24, 1973, her father's release date, of all the days to be late! Thanks in part to a public outcry, making Elmer Carter out to be a heroic vigilante, his expensive attorney was able to appeal and knock the charge down to second-degree manslaughter and release from jail, his sentence reduced to time served.

Getting the old poop to agree to plead guilty was not easy.

Him insisting that he was making a legal citizen's arrest of a war criminal. It was an honest mistake, not his fault. That goddamn Himmler was 1000 times worse than Mengele and Eichmann put together. They ought to be pinning a medal on him, not throwing him in a goddamn clink like a common criminal.

At long last, it was Gwen's turn. She filled her tank to the brim. Thank goodness for small favors, people were cool and civil today. No jerks cutting into line. No screaming, no fistfights.

On her way, running yellow lights but no reds, she reached the regional jail just in time.

No reporters hovered outside. Elmer Carter was old news.

The media and its short attention span had moved on locally to a mayoral scandal and sinkholes above an old mine damaging and destroying homes in a new development.

Beyond the city limits, news was the Arab oil embargo

and Watergate.

Seventy-two-year-old Elmer Carter had shockingly aged. On her weekly visits, under fluorescent lights, she'd observed a jailhouse pallor.

Out in the open, his skin was old leather and he trembled as he signed release papers. Sixteen-and-a-half months behind bars had tacked on five hard years. He had gone from a spry, mischievous oldster to Methuselah.

He'd acted hangdog at those visits, eyes downcast and speech barely audible.

Outside, a free man, he projected a trace of a swagger, as if freedom had energized him.

He asked where the hell the reporters were.

She told him he was vain and conceited for the wrong reasons.

He said they didn't deliver newspapers and the TV favorites were cartoons. You risked your life if you changed channels.

He'd been updated on every visit how loved ones were and had gotten letters, but he wanted a rehash.

Everyone and everything was fine, Gwen Carter told him.

A white lie.

On her visits, her father had been reluctant to speak of how it was for him on the *inside* and had changed the subject whenever she asked.

In the car, the facility out of sight, him looking in the passenger mirror to be sure, he launched into an unprompted war story.

It was rough at first, he said. Me a geezer in there with all these goddamn criminals. The coloreds, they have this black power thing and they're as mean as snakes.

Blacks, Dad.

Right, blacks. The whites, forget them too. You got your share of racist white trash inside. Me accidentally killing their hero making a citizen's arrest didn't win me any brownie points. With Nazi Newt gone, their merry band was fizzling out and they didn't like that too much.

That left me and a light-skinned colored boy who was more albino than mulatto. High yellow is what they used to call them.

Light-skinned *black man,* Dad.

Elmer said to clean out her ears, that's what he'd said. The two of them, they were the odd men out. Since he was a celebrity and the colored boy was a square peg in a round hole, so to speak, the screws babysat them.

Having us shower by ourselves for one, instead of with the general population. You heard about not dropping your soap in the jailhouse shower, haven't you?

She shook her head.

Good advice, he said, leaving it at that.

Gwen Carter said it sounded horrible in there.

Elmer Carter said it was no picnic, but things turned around for him.

How?

Pruno.

What?

Pruno. It's what you drink in the joint when single-malt Scotch and French wine aren't available, and there are none of those sommelier wine snob guys.

What?

No bar waitresses in short skirts. No white tablecloths.

No tinkling piano music.

Dad, what is pruno?

Pruno's made of *everything* you can ferment. Fresh fruit, catsup, bread, sauerkraut, sugar cubes, fruit cocktail.

Pruno aficionados don't have oak barrels at their disposal or patience. You mash it up in a plastic bag, heat the bag however you can. Running hot water over the bag works. Then let nature take its course. In a week it does.

Yuck.

Yuck for sure, but it's potent, which is all they care about. Word got out that they had a chemist in their midst with food and beverage savvy who could make the beverage tastier with an even higher octane rating.

You didn't.

If a request is made for service as an, ahem, scientific advisor, it is wise to accept the invitation.

Tell me you didn't, Dad.

Let us just say that our pruno was the envy of our fellow inmates, an outstanding vintage that could stand up to wino wine on the outside, the rotgut they drink out of paper bags.

Gwen let it pass.

As an alcoholic who would've drank lighter fluid in the bad old days if it maintained her buzz, she was no one to talk.

She measured her next words: Dad, you didn't shake before.

Eyes straight ahead: Let us say that it would be rude not to have a little taste at cocktail hour. Hey, what's up? This isn't the way to the mansion you live in with that slimy carpetbagger you shouldn't've married.

No, it isn't, she said.

She didn't say that the "mansion" was gone, sold at a bargain price to a senior vice-president in charge of technology at the company Laura worked for.

Laura, who served in the man's department two rungs below him, even though she knew twice as much.

Gwen said she didn't live with Bob and that their divorce would be final soon.

Elmer Carter raised a fist and said that he hoped that she'd taken the goddamn son of a bitch for every penny he had.

She evaded the remark by saying she was rattling around in that big house, so she moved into a really nice apartment with Mary Ann and Ocean, a townhouse layout. There's a bedroom and bath on the second level for you too, Dad.

He looked his daughter and asked if she was keeping an eye on him, which was bullshit if she was. Hell, he wasn't even on parole.

She smiled, saying that yes he was on parole and she was his parole officer.

Been seeing any nice fellas? Or not-so-nice fellas?

No, Dad. The male of the species can wait.

An outright lie.

They drove in silence, Gwen thinking about when she stopped for a cup of coffee this morning and gave the cashier a dollar bill that was upside down in her wallet. Her mind was constantly on money, primarily the lack of it, so she'd noticed the Great Seal and e pluribus unum on the bill.

Why she hadn't noticed the Great Seal and e pluribus

unum before and why she did now? Because Gwen Carter had money on her mind, Gwen Carter thought. Far too much. She vowed to put a stop to it.

Topnotch criminal defense lawyers were expensive, their fees in triple digits per hour. If her dad had been able to keep his mouth shut at his trial and hadn't rambled so much on the stand, a public defender could've gotten the same result.

So anxious was Gwen to be rid of the repulsive creature who was her lawfully-wedded husband, she signed away virtually all her assets but the house. The house a windfall for the senior vice-president.

On the plus side of the ledger, Bob Jones needed the money to pay *his* expensive lawyer to defend him.

To no avail.

The weasel was serving a sentence at a country-club prison for falsifying records and bilking the government out of millions of dollars on a failed weapon system. Jones Armament and Research was in receivership and its president and CEO was doing three years.

Yea!

Elmer Carter's home was vacant. She'd attempt to persuade him to sell it after the recession ended and housing prices rose, and to rent it out in the meantime. Good luck with that.

As if reading her mind, he asked if she'd been looking after his house.

She said she was on her visits and she still was.

Atta girl.

Don't waste your times looking for that box of bumper stickers.

The ones that came like a day before the Nazi fell down and broke his crown. You tossed them out, didn't you?

Gwen nodded.

How come?

You were going to stick them on bumpers, weren't you?

That's what bumper stickers are for, Gwen.

Whether the car owner wants one on or not?

People don't know what's good for them.

What's the point of THIS IS A BUMPER?

Awareness. They're close enough to read the sticker, they're too close to the bumper. Preventing rear-enders is the point. Putting Whiplash Willie in the unemployment line.

And SAVE THE PLANET. IT'S THE ONLY ONE WITH BEER?

Self-explanatory. Unless you know something the rest of us don't.

And IF THIS CAR WAS A GIFT, YOU GOT GYPPED?

Shames them into taking their goddamn beater off the road before it kills somebody. Shames them into jacking it up on blocks at their trailer park.

Good luck with that, she thought as she entered the apartment building's parking lot.

She also thought how blessed she was, living with loved ones and being sober for over seven-and-a-half years.

Truly blessed.

Blessed too for a man she was going to see after dropping Dad off and powdering her nose.

He was younger than her, a bartender even.

It began three years ago. She met him when a stress-induced craving came close to overwhelming her. The bar was across town, so there'd be little chance of running into somebody she knew.

She had gone in, sat at the bar, and ordered a whiskey sour and a package of cigarettes. The only way she thought she could beat the two-headed demon was going face-to-face with it.

She sat directly in front of the back bar and shelves of hard liquor. Recessed lighting caused the liquid in the transparent bottles to glow jewel-like.

Stupid, Gwen thought. She'd given herself insurmountable odds to defeat.

Custer's Last Stand.

She opened the cigarette pack, took one out and moved the whiskey sour closer.

Close enough to smell.

Gwen Carter took a deep breath, stood up, and tossed the cigarettes over the bar into a wastebasket, then emptied the sour into a sink.

She asked the bartender for a cup of coffee.

Black and strong, please.

It was a slow afternoon, so the bartender had time to talk after pouring Gwen's coffee. He wasn't especially handsome or fit. He had little ambition.

But he was a sweet man, beginning to gray.

She was the sort of man you could talk to and he'd listen.

She spoke of her problem and he spoke of his.

The bartender was a multiple DWI whose boozing

drove off his family. He liked her "face the twin demons" analogy. That was exactly what he was doing. He had taken this job and was now part owner of the bar.

He refilled Gwen's cup and said he was a boss and could take off whenever he liked.

She didn't reply.

Nervously, he said that if she liked, he'd have the night bartender come in early.

So they could go to his apartment.

As soon as he said it, he apologized for coming on so strong. He blurted it out because it was how he felt.

Gwen asked him how soon his replacement could get here.

From then on, the bartender was there for her when stress overwhelmed. No strings attached by either party.

Her outright lie.

Her secret.

EASY MONEY *wasn't. Those who worshipped at the Sacrament of Easy Money never learned.*

Case in point: Glen Carter, chronically-unemployed drifter and brother of Gwen Carter.

It was thirty minutes after midnight, the start of a new day, Tuesday, April 29, 1975.

Glen Carter, eyes at half-mast, did not know or care that the last Americans in South Vietnam were being evacuated by helicopter from the roof of the United States Embassy in Saigon. He didn't even know or care that Elvis Presley had performed that evening in Murfreesboro, Tennessee.

Glen Carter did not know or care about events beyond his own needs.

What he did know and care about was that the drunk six stools down the bar from him was close to passing out. Nicely dressed and in Glen's 50-something age range, he'd been in that shape when he staggered in half an hour before. The bartender had served him one drink, bourbon on the rocks that he downed in two sips, but now refused to serve him another.

The drunk called him a name and staggered back out.

Glen Carter had seen the drunk pay for the shot from a wallet stuffed with currency. Glen gulped down the rest of his draft beer, went outside, and saw the drunk stumble into an alley.

All was quiet, nobody out and about. Glen followed the drunk into the alley. Glen Free Carter was not a violent person. He'd like to be, but he was too cowardly.

Glen did not want bloodshed, specially his own.

He'd see what happened, what developed, was all.

Halfway through the alley, the drunk tried to hang on to a brick wall, but couldn't. Fingers attempting to cling, he slumped to his knees.

If the drunk hadn't passed out, he was close to it.

Glen Carter never ignored a shot at easy money, in spite of easy money *always* ignoring him. His luck was about to change.

He dropped to his knees behind the drunk and reached into his back pocket for the plump wallet.

Glen Carter's luck did change.

From bad to much worse.

The drunk grabbed Glen's wrist and yanked. Surprised and off-balance and three sheets to the wind himself, Glen slammed headfirst into the wall and fell on his back.

Another guy came out of nowhere and held a pocketknife to his throat.

The sober drunk took Glen's wallet, change and then his shoes, the latter to discourage pursuit.

Away the "drunk" and his partner went, running and laughing.

Glen Carter lay there, cold, sore and dazed, minus his only pair of shoes.

He was $23.46 poorer too.

And no wiser.

F

FIREWORKS *were not invented by Chinese people long long ago. Eight-year-old Quyen Wilson knew they hadn't been.*

She knew that fireworks and gunpowder came to us here in our world from the Planet Krypton. The rocket that landed didn't have baby Superman in it. If it did, where was the Man of Steel?

She read the funny pages every day. She looked and looked in the sky and never saw him leaping tall buildings in a single bound.

Where was Superman if he was really real?

She knew what was really in the rocket. Gunpowder and the recipe for fireworks was. That was where fireworks came from. It was. She knew a lot of things nobody else knew she knew.

She read better than anybody knew she read. She could read numbers and words in the newspapers Daddy and Mommy and Gramma Gwen read.

She knew numbers and words like seven shot dead in robbery, 41 killed in explosion, 88 killed in rocket attack.

Gunpowder and fireworks killed people. They killed people in wars. She didn't quite grasp what a war was, but she knew it had to be the worst thing there was. She had heard many fireworks in a war, even though she didn't know what a war was and didn't remember hearing them.

She just knew she had.

Jim Wilson knelt by his daughter's bed holding her hand. The entire house was dark on Sunday July 4, 1976, the nation's Bicentennial Day.

It was twilight outside on this, one of the longest days of the year, but the Wilsons had darkened their home further by closing drapes and blinds, and shut off all lights except a night light in the bathroom.

Only a quarter of a mile from their home in a park, a fireworks show was slated to begin at sundown. It wasn't as lavish as the one in the city, but the Wilsons would be able to see it if they wished and hear it even if they didn't.

Jim liked the dark too. He liked isolation, he liked being unseen. He was happy to stay in the BREAD warehouse forever.

Had he taken the slide rule company's pity job, it was gone now anyway.

Gone with the slide rule company.

Thanks to the pocket calculator, the slide rule joined the stagecoach and kerosene lantern in technological oblivion.

Jim liked isolation and darkness because he didn't want people to see him. His panache had faded. Even though the Vietnam War was over and Saigon was Ho Chi Minh City, people gave him sidelong stares, him a casualty in a stupid and futile war, a freak with his missing eye and fingers and his scars. Scars he couldn't completely cover without wearing an overcoat, ski mask, and gloves.

Worse, people avoided looking at all.

The fireworks show was underway, popping and booming and flashing. Light blinked through the drapes and inadequately filtered the noise.

Quyen threw her arms around her father and mother, and they held her. This fear of the sight and sound of vicarious warfare must be imprinted, the Wilsons believed. The child was simply too young to recall the real deal.

It wasn't as bad as the Fourth of July last year, Laura Wilson thought. Quyen had screamed herself hoarse. It wasn't the best night for Jim Wilson either. At the sound of the first cherry bomb, he damn near jumped out of his shoes.

Quyen had stopped hiding food in her room too, setting part of her dinner aside, folding it in napkins when she thought they weren't looking.

Every night after their daughter had gone to sleep, they'd find it in her room. Broccoli, rice, chicken, macaroni and cheese, anything that had been on her plate, foods she liked *and* disliked.

Quyen's curiosity of things inside her home and outside grew by the day. The area behind the car in her mother and father's garage that her mother had made into a workshop/office fascinated her.

Watching her mother working in her spare time at the workbench was as entertaining as TV cartoons.

She even liked the smell of hot solder.

Laura doubted that Quyen understood much of what she was doing, building a prototype with an old black-and-white television she'd bought as a garage sale for five dollars.

The old portable typewriter she'd taken apart for the

keys and mechanism.

Wiring like spaghetti all over the place.

Those weird things that Laura told Quyen were circuit boards and chips.

Chips that weren't at all like potato chips and corn chips.

Chips you couldn't eat.

A *chip* off the old block, Laura Wilson thought, as they held their little girl tighter as the fireworks grew louder and brighter.

≈≈≈

Six-year-old Ocean Benson had no fear of fireworks. He'd been counting the days until the Fourth of July. Along with his mother and Gramma Gwen, they packed snacks and drinks, going early to assure themselves a prime vantage point on a bluff.

Entranced, Ocean took in the display.

The whistling rockets.

The sky lit up by sparkling fountains.

He knew about Quyen and fireworks, but didn't understand why scared her.

It made him sad that they did.

≈≈≈

Elmer Carter stayed home on Bicentennial Day. As far as he was concerned, this Fourth of July folderol was as big a pain in the ass as Christmas, except that it lasted one day and the goddamn lead-up to Christmas went on for weeks.

After the gang left for their firecracker thing, he knelt beside the kitchen sink and reached way in the back where he hid his whiskey. It was behind some cleaning stuff so old that the caps were rusted on.

He dug out the fifth, half empty now. Pruno or no pruno, when he was in the joint he was no lush. So how come Gwen made a federal case out of it if he wanted a little taste? It was a helluva lot easier to have a hit while they were out of the house so he didn't have to go through the goddamn Spanish Inquisition.

Elmer liked his bourbon neat. For a shot glass, he poured some into one of those jars they used for juice glasses, the ones soft cheese came in.

He lifted his glass and his throat burned. It wasn't the smoothest booze on the market, but he hadn't taken a sip yet.

His throat burned and his chest was clamped in a vise.

He smelled burning leaves.

He was thinking that *every* religion exists because we cannot accept the finality of death. They were all the same, every last one of them.

So don't let those TV preachers and fanatics that hand out pamphlets con you into playing along with them.

Then he didn't taste or smell or think anything.

≈≈≈

Bob Jones did not take in a fireworks show on Bicentennial day.

He had 21 days left to serve on his three-year sentence. Twenty-one long days in this "country club" institution.

Unfairly locked up for being what the media cynically termed the Flea Killer Edison.

He regarded "county club" as a sick joke. Oh sure, they had dormitories, workout rooms, tennis courts, and swimming pools.

And the “residents” dressed in khakis and pullovers, for a casual look.

His dorm also had a resident by the name of *Mister* Higgins, as Jones was ordered to address him.

Mr. Higgins was a beady-eyed bond analyst who stood 6’6” and weighed 345 pounds. Mr. Higgins was bisexual, bipolar, schizophrenic and psychotic.

A child molester too and proud of it.

But Mr. Higgins had not been incarcerated for pedophilia.

In Bob Jones’ opinion, he should have been convicted and sentenced to life for pedophilia, not for the only blot on his record, a wire fraud conviction for which he was doing 18 months.

Mr. Higgins was infatuated with Bob Jones. He’d fallen hard for Bob. He made smooching sounds, telling Bob he was his middle-aged Adonis and his sweetie pie.

Bob Jones despised homos, in prison or out. They were sick and disgusting. But the man would not take no for an answer. As fine a physical specimen as Bob was, working out in the country club’s weight room, he was no match for the massive lust-crazed pervert.

Consequently, Bob Jones became Mr. Higgins’ bitch.

It was not Bob’s nature to report the problem to those in charge. He was used to being in charge and, too, if he snitched, he’d have a fatal accident in this country club penal institution.

Perhaps in the weight room or the swimming pool.

Guaranteed.

He could stand on his head for 21 more days.

So when the degenerate nudged him awake with a tap

on the neck with his shank after lights-out and called him Sweetie and said it was time to rock and roll, Bob Jones resignedly got out of bed.

The deviant's shank was constructed of a razor blade inserted into a toothbrush handle and bound with tape. A shank was a primitive weapon, but in the event Bob wasn't in a romantic mood, it'd make short work of his carotid artery.

The couple went into the latrine. Their dorm mates knew that the latrine was off-limits until the end of their assignation.

Bent over a sink, the animal thrusting inside him, Bob Jones swore yet again to catch whoever blew the whistle on ARMAGEDDON X7, ruining his life.

The perv was biting his neck and slobbering, squeezing him even harder.

The sign that he was almost done.

Twenty-one more days.

≈≈≈

Although he was a well-paid federal employee, presumably a patriotic American, Bicentennial Day remained an abstraction to Roscoe Snails.

His mind was on his assignment, to play a tourist in the State of Georgia, not an easy role for one so serious. As with his June 10, 1972 Watergate break-in and subsequent tasks, Roscoe's orders came from a *someone.*

A peanut farmer, Georgia's former governor was the favorite to win the presidential nomination in less than two weeks at the Democratic National Convention.

The peanut farmer had an eccentric family.

A drunken brother who owned a gas station.

A sister who was a faith healer.

Roscoe Snails rented a car at the Atlanta airport and set out to obey his nebulous instructions to learn what he could learn of this family, whatever that was.

More often than not, he drilled a dry hole.

But one of these days –

FREE WIL I. *Specifications: Polished wood case holding a keyboard. Inside, 50 chips (not potato or corn), a 4KB memory expandable to 48 KB. Character graphics with 20 x 40 resolution.*

$599.95, monitor not included.

Saturday December 31, 1976. The Wilsons' New Year's Eve party at their home centered on the dining room and the garage. The buffet and drinking on the dining table, the garage as venue for the 11:59 PM champagne toast. All Wilsons attended.

The twins, David Junior and Richard, recent mechanical engineering grads and a world of help to Laura on FREE WIL I, were going to have their first glass of French champagne.

Jim and Laura thought his kid brothers were peculiar in a way hard to pin down. They still dressed identically. Junior and Richard had filled out too, their faces roundish like their mother's. They had become cigarette smokers, a sophisticated affectation for the university man.

Gwen and Mary Ann were there.

Ocean was there, in bed with Quyen, both sound asleep, a radio on elevator music set at low volume, but high enough to drown out celebratory fireworks.

The Wilsons had spent some money updating their home to keep in tune with 1970s chic. Avocado appliances. Shag carpeting. Dark, wood-grained paneling. Beanbag chairs. The obligatory lava lamps.

The Wilsons were fashionable too, polyestered to the nines, each in bellbottoms. Jim's hair was de rigueur: muttonchops and a bushy moustache. Laura had counted 19 stitched cuts out of the 512 covered by facial hair.

Per her mental calculation, 3.71 % of them.

Gwen proposed the toast, her glass of root beer raised. To everybody's health and wealth and happiness.

The rest raised their champagne glasses and they toasted one another, clinking glasses to Laura's exciting new venture and the product she hoped was the leading edge of a computer in the average American's home.

Other companies were entering this new market, so why not her? When she clinked Gwen's, she wordlessly thanked her mommy for the investment that put her over the top on FREE WIL I – a grubstake for material and parts for more units, and advertising.

Her father's will left his home and the scant other assets to Gwen, leaving Glen, his ne'er-do-well son a goose egg.

Gwen had been fortunate to sell the large, luxurious house in a down market for $72,995. The lion's share was pumped into her daughter's FREE WIL, Inc.

At 12:05 AM, January 1, 1977, after the fireworks petered out and Jim checked to see that the kids were asleep, they drank a solemn toast to the memory of Elmer F. Carter, who had been honored in the naming of FREE WIL, Inc., his middle name and the first syllable of Laura's last name.

To a wonderful father, grandfather, great grandfather, and human being, who was unjustly punished for ridding the planet of a hatemonger.

All glasses lifted, not a dry eye in the house.

≈≈≈

Bob Jones was not celebrating the New Year.

He had a few drinks, though.

His drinking companion was having more than a few.

His companion who was crying in his beer that he hadn't garnered a Pulitzer nomination for his exposé of Jones Armament and Research, and the ARMAGEDDON X7 fiasco.

On his own, Bob Jones made no headway identifying the individual who ruined his life. Employees of the defunct Jones Armament had dispersed.

Bob Jones exhausted a double-digit percentage of the money he'd squirreled away in Swiss and offshore accounts, paying private detectives to chase down the employees.

The shamuses located the majority and wrote extensive reports without knowing why.

Bob Jones read the reports and concluded that none were culpable.

Bob took an oblique approach and contacted the ace reporter/muckraker who broke the X7 story, saying he held no hard feelings against the journalist.

The journalist was speechless.

However, Bob was bitter that he had to take the fall alone.

Alone?

There were others who concealed the project's failures. Concealed it criminally.

After a pause: Why didn't that come out at your trial?

There was no proof. They covered their tracks too well.

Bob had new information, new names. A crack reporter like you could unearth the truth. Justice would be served.

The reporter's vanity overrode his suspicions. He met

Bob Jones for drinks and more drinks, everything he wanted on Bob.

Bob revealed tidbits of the private eyes' accounts.

The reporter took notes, asked questions, chain-smoked and drank.

Bob named every employee who the PIs couldn't find and those who'd been in management positions, a total of 19.

The reporter asked no questions about any, nor offered comments.

He did flutter a dismissive hand at one name: Roscoe Snails.

If Snails was adamantly above the reporter's suspicion, therefore he was The One.

Roscoe Snails aka Judas Iscariot.

The Flea Killer Edison.

≈≈≈

In the early hours of the New Year, Bob Jones sat in his car, parked catty-corner from Roscoe's posh townhouse. He glanced at his Rolex to confirm that 1977 had arrived. The year made no difference to Bob Jones, it was just a number.

The ostentatious gold Rolex reminded him who he was, who he vowed to be again.

He waited for Roscoe's lights to go out, or for someone to come or go. He was going to be his own private eye.

He wasn't yet certain what he was going to do, other than give Mr. Roscoe Benedict Arnold Vidkun Quisling Snails a bad day.

A very bad day.

He wondered why Snails betrayed him.

Hadn't he compensated Roscoe well?

It couldn't be because he was fucking Mary Ann Snails, the slut. Roscoe's ex was getting it from every guy in town and got careless, popping out a bastard son.

Roscoe Snails was creepy-weird, impossible to read, but there had to be a cogent reason.

Had to be.

G

GERUND. *A verbal noun ending in –ing. The name of Venus' second moon.*

Gerund was discovered on April 7, 1978 by 32-year-old Jim Wilson, an amateur astronomer looking through a telescope he'd paid $199.95 for with money he'd saved from his paper route.

On that day, prior to Gerund's discovery, 10-year-old Quyen Wilson came home from school with homework that stumped her. This was highly unusual. The fifth grader was in accelerated classes for all her subjects.

Quyen told her father she had an English assignment she comprehended, but did not understand.

Upon making peace with his masculine pride, Jim Wilson had accepted the role of househusband. He'd accepted his appearance too. To an extent, aided by ample facial hair. Darkness wasn't mandatory, but he did prefer to stay in the nest.

Free Wil, Inc. was going gangbusters. Laura had moved from the garage to a business park five miles from home. Laura had nine employees – an office staff plus techies. Loans allowed all to be paid salaries.

Of those in design and assembly, her brothers-in-law, the Wilson twins, and a college pal of theirs, a whiz kid at writing computer code, stood out.

Mary Ann worked part-time, keeping the books. She'd

recently taken some accounting classes.

Partner Gwen pitched in too when she had ample volunteers at BREAD to spell her, sweet and smooth on the phone to local radio and TV stores, asking them to stock their products. She'd cajoled the editor of an electronics magazine to send out a reporter for the launch next week of FREE WIL II.

At the dining room table with Quyen, Jim hoped he could help her quickly. In 15 minutes it was time to pick up Ocean so Mary Ann could go to work. Jim took him to soccer practice on those days.

Ocean lived for soccer, a game that wasn't around for kids when Jim was a kid, a game where nobody but the goalkeepers used their hands.

It'd frustrate Jim, but eight-year-old Ocean was the team's star defender, on a team of predominantly nine-year-olds. It was Friday and they'd be sleeping over at Mary Ann's and Gwen's.

Okay, he said, checking her homework sheet and textbook. Here's an example. Play*ing* tennis is fun. You try one.

She smiled, catching on instantly. Quyen learned English by listening and speaking. Not by writing page after page of conjugated verbs, the rote that made Jim despise foreign language classes.

Play*ing* soccer is fun for Ocean.

Her dad smiled. C'mon, kiddo. Too easy. Too much like the example.

It took her five seconds to come up with: we are danc*ing*, runn*ing* fast is tir*ing*, jump*ing* high is exhilarat*ing*.

Problem solved.

≈≈≈

It took Laura much more than five seconds to regain her composure. She was on the verge of turning the air blue. Motherhood and the absence of Father Sir had moderated her urge to swear. Except on rare instances such as now.

In the restroom, door locked.

Shit piss fuck shit piss fuck shit piss fuck shit piss fuck shit piss fuck!

Vented now, she thought of how reliable Richard Wilson was reworking schematics and on the assembly line.

Rock solid.

Past tense.

The line came to a screeching halt when the last units didn't work. Richard had transposed two chips in 11 of the 75.

Units that *had to be* done for next week's roll out.

She firmly believed that the company's success or failure hinged upon II's.

Every week there was a new competitor in the marketplace.

No. A new competitor every *day*.

A shy young man, Richard was doubtlessly a virgin. Laura had inadvertently placed him in the proximity of the girl he was now going with, a coquettish little blonde with big hair named Kelli.

Kelli who Laura sized up as a tease with a talent for making the blood in Richard's brain rush to his dick. Her obvious objective was holy matrimony (i.e. financial security).

Kelli who signed the "i" with a bubble, not the standard dot, a cautionary tale in itself. But Free Wil's rapid growth required new employees immediately, if not sooner.

Kellı^{o}, who Laura had fired, but not before the damage was done.

An unemployed elevator operator, Kelli was a secretary/typist/stenographer at Free Wil, Inc. In job description only.

Laura Wilson could type faster with her toes than the bimbo could with her fingers. Kelli's best office skill was crossing and recrossing her legs as she swiveled in her chair. Laura didn't know and didn't want to know what Richard saw in her and inside her short-short skirts.

Oh wait, of course she knew.

It was lust at first sight.

She was tempted to buy Richard a piece of tail.

Have Laura's purchase come to Richard's apartment door in leotards and plunging neckline, a new neighbor borrowing a cup of sugar, one thing leading to another, the C12H22O11 forgotten.

He'd get his horns clipped and not make a horrible mistake.

She'd have a dependable employee again.

Thinking about sex made Laura think of Jim. Her 70-hour weeks hadn't been terrific for their love life. She'd call him right away, saying that they had the house to themselves tonight.

As she reached for the receiver, her phone rang, Jim saying, hey, they have the house to ourselves tonight.

She said they were telepathic and took the rest of the afternoon off.

After his soccer and sleepover errands, Jim walked in the door to a darkened house. Candles were lit at the dining table, a bottle of wine opened. He looked at Laura in her negligee and said that the wine needed more time to breathe.

In bed, they had a quick discussion on who'd be on top, who'd be on the bottom.

They compromised.

Him on the bottom in bed, her on the bottom in the back seat of the 1962 Chevrolet Impala SS convertible.

After they wore each other out, Laura Wilson snored contentedly in bed.

Jim Wilson put on a robe, tiptoed out of the bedroom, poured a glass of wine, and went out to the patio to a crisp, starry night. Venus dominated the sky. He aimed his trusty old telescope and aimed it at The Evening Star and (hopefully) fickle Aphrodite.

Oh my God oh my God oh my God oh my God oh my God oh my God oh my God oh my God, there she was!!!!!!

♥o

The Venusian moon was there and it was gone.

Aphrodite was different — a solid black heart that had a light spot, a circular spot on an edge.

A pin prick, gleaming in contrast as if a diamond.

A mile in diameter?

Five miles? No larger than that.

Had he seen what he'd seen? Not spots in front of his eyes?

Yes he had. He'd seen a hot spot, a reflection grazing

Aphrodite. He had seen Venus's second moon.

There'd been strong solar flare activity lately. Jim surmised that a monster of a flare, one 1000 or 2000 miles high, the power of a zillion H-bombs, had illuminated whatever it illuminated at an optimum angle.

He knew what he'd seen, and that's how he wanted to tell his story.

He started a letter on a FREE WIL II Laura had brought home. It was in the garage hooked up to a brand-new daisy wheel printer. He did not, however, name Venus's second moon.

Anointing the first Aphrodite had been a mistake. Though he didn't know for certain, he figured he'd been deemed as childish and presumptuous. He didn't know for certain because his letters were never answered.

He *had* to tell Laura.

He awakened her with kisses and told his story.

He said he changed his mind and wasn't going to contact observatories and universities. To hell with it. To hell with them.

Laura took him by a hand and led him into to the garage.

She said to keep writing your letter, to hell what the so-called experts thought if he named Venus's second moon. Them and their advanced degrees and their giant planetariums and their symposiums and their learned papers.

Regardless, Jim said. To them, he was a joke, a crank, an obsessed crackpot.

Fuck them and the horse they rode in on, she said. Get those letters done and printed and in the mail.

Naming your discovery too.
Gerund.
Gerund it was.
Aphrodite and Gerund. A nice ring to it.
He finished his letter and printed 50 copies.
Off they'd go to the same old places.
They can believe him or not.

GRILLED CHEESE SANDWICH. *An ancient food that took many forms, so said historians. The modern American version appeared in the 1920s. Sliced bread and American cheese were inexpensive then. The grilled cheese sandwich was popular during the Great Depression.*

Images of the Virgin Mary had been seen on grilled cheese sandwiches.

How special was that?

The grilled cheese sandwich was the zenith of Roscoe Snails' culinary achievements.

Preceding her hippie phase and descent into a life as a tramp, Mary Ann was a satisfactory cook who'd make June Cleaver proud. She did American classics like pot roast, meatloaf, and chicken and dumplings.

For dinner parties, she'd competently explore the fringes of gourmet. Chicken Kiev, bœuf bourguignon, osso buco.

On this evening of Saturday April 8, 1978, home and famished, Roscoe Snails started his dinner. Organization and preparation were the keys, on the job and off duty.

Number one was a fine Andalucían sherry, lush and brimming with fruit, open on the counter to breathe.

Roscoe's was no mundane grilled cheese sandwich like those served to public schoolchildren. He greased the pan with extra virgin olive oil. The bread was marbled rye, the cheese Shilton™.

He opened the fridge for the cheese.

The 1/100 of a second he had to live was not time enough to be annoyed that the refrigerator light had burned out.

The light had not burned out.

There was no light.

Two wires ran from the light's socket to a grayish lump on the top shelf by a jar of raspberry jam.

Someone had entered while he was gone, unplugged the fridge, removed the light, ran the two wires from the socket to a gob of *plastique*, closed the door, and plugged the fridge back in.

The refrigerator door and Roscoe Snails smashed through the front wall and window into the chargé d'affaires of an impoverished landlocked nation.

The diplomat lived in and ran a consulate in a townhouse across the street. He'd been on the sidewalk in front of the Snails residence, walking his Lhasa apso.

Man and beast were killed instantaneously by flying pieces of masonry, glass, refrigerator door, and Roscoe Snails.

The times were sensitive, as all times were sensitive. Roscoe's employers managed to have the double homicide swept under the carpet as a gas-line explosion.

The deceased chargé d'affaires' impoverished nation was given a grant and the expertise to build a coal-fired electrical-generation plant in a razed slum near its capital city.

Bob Jones would come to think of the late diplomat in that Vietnam-inspired neologism, *collateral damage*.

Roscoe Snails had no next of kin. He was cremated and his ashes were dumped down a drain.

At the time of the explosion, Bob sat in an upscale lounge two blocks away, enjoying a glass of an intriguing ten-year-old Malbec. He didn't rush out to the sidewalk to see what had happened as other patrons did.

He knew what had happened.

The only surprise was the strength of the explosion. It sounded as if lightning had struck the brushed stainless-steel bar. He'd never worked with *plastique,* so he erred on the side of caution by using too much rather than too little.

Bob Jones was a patient man. Since learning the truth about Roscoe and reconnoitering his townhouse on New Year's Day, he knew what he had to do.

Today is the first day of the rest of my life.

That moronic 1970s truism hung with him like a hemorrhoid.

In preparation, Bob Jones had enrolled in a locksmithing course in a different state under a different name.

Upon graduation, he got in touch with a jailbird colleague, a gastroenterologist who had been caught swindling Medicare.

The gastroenterologist had spoken bitterly of a first cousin and safecracker who'd done time. The cracksman had been the black sheep of the family until passing the torch to the good doctor.

The defrocked gastroenterologist was working as a veterinary assistant.

Bob asked him to arrange a meeting with the safecracker.

The doctor balked until Bob offered him a fee that was "more than you make in three months cleaning dogshit out of cages."

The safecracker swore he'd reformed, as if Bob cared. He did agree to check with an old crony to see if had a line on tools and supplies of the trade, specifically explosives.

For a price.

Listening to sirens, Bob Jones lifted his glass to request a refill.

He toasted himself in the back bar mirror.

One down.

HIGHTOWER.

First name: Buster.

Middle name: none.

Occupation: Stand-up comic.

Shtick: Ranting and raving, a maniacal outrage over politics and other trivia. No cruelty, no obscenity. You want the f-word, he'd tell them, go in the can and read what's scratched in the wall above the urinal. No racism, no misogyny, no potty humor for Buster Hightower either.

Résumé: The periphery of his profession. Retirement parties and wakes and second-tier comedy clubs. Whistle-stopping from saloon to smoker to bachelor party to corporate retreat to dumpy casino to NCO club.

To company picnics, where he was now.

Hey, a show of hands. How many of you are happy that Watergate and the Watergating crooks are done and gone, out of the news?

I'm counting 15 or 20 hands, counting the show of both hands. Okay, you're exercising your constipational right to cast a voter's ballot in this great nation of ours. Me, I'd be sitting on my hands if I wasn't standing up, mike in one hand, ice cold bottle of the beer in the other.

Know why? Today's what? Saturday, August 13, 1980.

Back in the very good old days, on a Saturday too,

June 17, 1972, five crooks who couldn't break into their own homes with the front door wide open, they got nabbed by a Watergate security guard.

Simultaneous-like, I broke into the profession at a motel lounge in Toledo, Ohio.

So I got a soft spot in my heart and head for the scandal. I'm only sorry it didn't go on longer.

Watergate was a cash cow for me and a kazillion comics. Yeah, it was.

I'd shift the mike from one hand to the other as I shifted from snarling Senate subcommittee interrogator to weaseling unindicted coconspirator.

Great fun and the audiences lapped it up.

Kinda dull these days in the news. You got your wars in Africa and those other countries over there. You got your floods and your droughts. You got your national overthrows and playoff sports teams overthrowing their opponents. Where's a good juicy scandal when you really need one?

I know these current and uncurrent events I'm getting you current on are glazing your eyeballs. That one gent in the back, he's snoring in his potato salad. Somebody rescue him so he doesn't potato salads' hisself to death. It'd be a horrible way to go.

Speaking of potato salad, it's as American as apple pie and beer and prime rib and beer. We all know that and we know potato salad's got eggs in it. This I don't know and maybe you can help me out, how come eggs are sold by the dozen? Why not by the 10 or 14 or some other number?

Doughnuts come by the dozen and that I can understand. A dozen doughnuts is a good start. But eggs?

A dozen is an even number is all I can figure. Do chickens lay eggs in pairs? That explains a little part of it, but not my whole entire question.

I'm not seeing any raised hands or anybody piping up with the answer. That's okay. This is a picnic. It ain't a quiz show or police interrogation.

Hey, you know those childproof containers we been seeing a lot of? Anybody else have trouble getting the things open? Yeah, you and you and you. Know what I do? I hire a child to open them. They're the only ones who can. The tykes work cheap too, charging me just a few pills out of the bottle.

Speaking of potato salad and the legal profession, I know of a lawyer who billed 28 hours of work a day, eight days a week. He's a sure thing for the Lawyer Hall of Fame. He'll be eligible to be voted in five years after retirement. He's spending those five years in a federal prison. The disbarred lawyer gets out with a new suit and 25 bucks. The hall of famer will have a certificate and a trophy waiting for him too.

Speaking of the hall of fame, why ain't Moe Mentum a member of the football one? Moe's played in every game I ever seen on TV on both teams. Moe switches from one team to another when they move the ball and score points. Poor guy never gets a rest. Is that unfair or what?

You got your political correctness these days, you know. Where the hell did that come from? A guy don't obey the PC rules, he's got the feminist police all over him.

So how come manhole covers get a pass? Why don't they have to be person-covers? It's discrimination against cast iron is what it is.

Same with mankind, management, manhandlers, manicurists, mannequins, and maniacs. If I was a gal, my nose'd be seriously out of joint.

You know, there're shopping malls sprouting up like crabgrass. I know this's not the season to be jolly, but malls remind me of Christmas. They're intertangled, right?

You may not know this, but Santa and his elves don't begin manufacturing or woman-facturing Xmas presents on the day after Thanksgiving. Blackbeard Friday, I think they call it. No way could they. They're hard at work as I speak to meet this year's demand.

I gotta feel for those elves up there at the North Pole. I gotta wonder about them too. Poor little guys, they oughta be unionized. You know they're making less than minimum wage and get no bennies.

Don't even think about workplace accidents in Santa's factory. They punch the time clock and walk home after a long long day. I have it on good authority that they come down with frostbite all the time. The frostbite-medicine pills they get, they can't open the bottles as they're tiny little adults, not kids.

You think Watergate was a cover-up? It's same-same and more with Santa's elves being eaten by polar bears.

You know that old ad slogan you'd see on commercials, Better Living Through Chemistry? Forget about medicine and chemical warfare, if chemistry is such a hot deal, how come they can't have themselves a breakthrough that's important, like geneticalistically engineering celery to taste like chocolate. There's a Nobel Prize in Betty Crockering waiting to be had.

Since I'm up here yakkety-yakking at a computer

company picnic, I oughta state my opinion on them machines, no offense I hope taken. Not too much offensiving taken.

I know I'm speaking blasphemy and am likely to lose the $1.98 fee I'm getting for appearing here with you nice folks. I hate to break the bad news. The contraptions are a fad. Yeah, they are.

Like backgammon's a big-deal fad now too. I hear tell they got backgammon computer games. Same with chess. You're playing these games on TV sets that you call your monotonies, right?

Now answer me one question. How the hell do the backgammon and chess pieces stick to the screen? As they gotta obey the law of gravity like anything else, don't they drop and fall off?

≈≈≈

Laura Wilson laughed and joined the crowd, putting their hands together for Buster Hightower.

The comic was a lucky find. Free Wil, Inc. had 75 employees and was growing out of their second location this year, the entire three stories of an industrial-park building.

FREE WIL III was three times as fast and powerful as FREE WIL II, and 500 times as fast and powerful as AZZTOUND 2111D.

Laura Wilson and Gwen Carter were multimillionaires on paper. They hung on to most of their shares, not selling them to a long line of eager buyers. Employees were allowed to purchase company stock also, the number of shares based on seniority. Many did, believing in the company's future.

Laura hosted company functions four times a year. They were welcome respites for her and Gwen too. Between the company and BREAD, free time was virtually unheard of.

Last quarter was bowling. Free Wil, Inc. reserved half the lanes in the alley. Laura heard laughter in the cocktail lounge, racked her ball, and looked in.

This comic, Buster Hightower, was performing on a rickety platform they'd erected for him between the dart board and cigarette machine. He was playing to a crowd of 15.

Not exactly headlining at a Vegas casino.

Hightower was tall, with wild hair and the makings of a spare tire. He might be 35, he might be 55.

He was outrageously funny.

Laura approached him afterward regarding the picnic.

Yeah, he'd said. He'd love to. His dance card was open. Don't even have to consult my appointment book.

Saying the last with a goofy, never-take-me-serious grin.

She'd scheduled him for a ridiculously low fee. Plus all the beer he could drink.

He'd said it'd be safe to bring children or anybody else, no problem. She'd rented a private park for the picnic. The kids weren't taking in his act. Ocean and Quyen and the rest were burning off unlimited energy in the play area.

Her Jim's attention was split between the comic and the kids playing. He was paying unusually close attention to them, on the verge of rudeness to the comic.

Ocean and Quyen were in no peril whatsoever, but you couldn't tell that by Jim's demeanor.

Overprotective of them.

How sweet.

Laura Wilson tried hard not to overshadow him, a househusband, who seemed to be content in the role.

They lived in the same three-bedroom, one bath rambler (that was paid off). Their lives were even-keeled and she did her damndest to keep it that that way.

≈≈≈

Yes, Jim Wilson knew the kids were in no peril whatsoever.

No, he could not stop paying unusually close attention to them.

Not after yesterday.

Jim had taken Ocean and Quyen out to a fast-food restaurant for lunch. They hadn't been there and wanted to try it, attracted to the colorful marquis. Technicolor plastic, he thought, a strong magnet to children.

They were at a table, digging into burgers and fries and soda. Quyen couldn't concentrate, her eyes darting from Ocean to the counter to her food.

Jim looked and knew why. At the rear counter where the manufactured food was placed in plasticware for hungry diners, a man twice the age of any of the adolescent help stood by. He was obese and his beady eyes were fixed on Ocean.

Jim Wilson read Quyen's fear.

His little girl recognized *evil.*

From her time in the womb she had.

Jim fixed his eye on the beady-eyed man.

Whose eyes met his eye.

A smallish man with an eye patch, missing two fingers,

and wearing scar tissue as if he'd been stitched together like a quilt, Jim Wilson would kill to prevent harm to these children.

That resolve made him twice as big and strong as the beady-eyed giant.

The prospective molester knew it too.

He averted his eyes and went into the back room.

≈≈≈

As she applauded Buster Hightower, it dawned on Laura why he worked so cheap.

The comic was G-rated, as he'd proudly stated, persona non grata to the majority of venues that demanded otherwise.

Poor man, his appeal had been stunted from Day One.

Mr. Hightower would have a sizable bonus in his check.

≈≈≈

Bob Jones would not have found the comic amusing. Not much tickled his funny bone. The last time he was amused was when Roscoe Snails opened his refrigerator door two-and-a-half years ago.

That was a riot!

Laura, who'd hired a comic, she was the clincher. She sickened him. The ungrateful little bitch he'd fed and clothed, who gotten knocked up by a pencil-necked loser, and miscarried. The loser's defective seed surely at fault for that and her hysterectomy.

Depriving Bob of the chance for a natural heir, Bob Jones Junior. Not leaving well enough alone, his daughter had to bring a gook kid into her family.

Her family, not his.

Adding insult to injury, she did not visit him *one fucking time* in those long three years at the penal "country club", going through a living hell as Mr. Higgins's bitch.

Now she was a mini-tycoon by the looks of it, a three-floor building in a suburban office complex, every square foot of it.

Her and The Queen of Whiskey Sours, her partner in Free Wil, Inc.

Bob tried in vain to put that connection into sharp focus. It logically went beyond mother and child linkage.

We were talking big bucks here, big and getting bigger.

Gwen didn't have a technical bone in her body. When she was on the sauce, she couldn't cap a whiskey bottle without crossing the threads.

Bob Jones, a patient man, waited for Laura's company's picnic. In comparison to Bob, the biblical Job was impulsive. Bob had not wasted the two-and-a-half years. He'd compiled dossiers on victims to come. Retribution for the three who'd wronged him.

Roscoe Snails.

Gwen Carter Jones.

Mr. Higgins.

While not a direct order, it was strongly implied that all Free Wil employees were to attend the picnic, even the workaholics there seven days a week.

Utilizing his tools and his locksmith training, in he went through a side door. The upper two floors were devoted to records and manufacturing. The main floor was open, all cubicles, even Gwen's and Laura's.

So what that their cubicles were slightly larger? The

egalitarian layout disgusted him. What were they trying to prove? That they were utopian socialists in capitalists' clothing?

Laura's concession to her exalted position was an antique wooden desk. Bob Jones knew this and knew the interior and the employees by memory, by visualization. He'd chatted up Free Wil workers at nearby watering holes, drinks on him, a gregarious and generous stranger. Half a dozen liked their beer and whiskey. Oddballs all, the more they drank, the more they boasted.

Bob brought prostitutes in, introducing them as family friends, cousins, whomever. Funny how the oddballs and the ladies invariably hit it off.

Oddballs who couldn't get the time of day from a homely woman.

Minutes later, in the back lot, love at first sight, they couldn't help themselves, the smitten lady's legs in the air, panties dangling from a toe, the automobile gently rocking.

The naïve, malleable, unquestioning oddballs loved the stranger and the free booze and the "dates" he provided.

They talked and talked.

The layout of Free Wil, who sat where, office politics, the picnic, anything he asked.

The world's oldest profession assisting in intelligence gathering, Bob thought.

An implement of spies for centuries.

For millennia.

No high tech like *plastique* and clever wiring this time. Bob had a pack of cigarettes, a lighter, and a small can of automotive grease. He went to his unappreciative daughter's desk. Wastebaskets were overflowing with wadded-up paper. A common boast by computer proponents was that the devices were the forefront of a paperless society.

Not yet. Not here.

He'd kill numerous birds with one stone. Gwen, for one, will need her own do-gooder charity, BREAD, to put food on her own table.

And Laura?

Not even Bob Jones could kill his own child.

Anyway, killing her dream was far more satisfying than killing her.

Bob disabled the fire alarm. It was done for monthly inspections, the knowledge courtesy of an oddball who was the safety monitor.

Bob opened the cigarette pack and the grease can. Laura's desk was kindling waiting to happen. Directly overhead was the mail room and the file room, with documents and envelopes piled willy-nilly.

He was going to grease the front side, shove a waste basket against it, and drop a lighted cigarette in. On his path out, he lit up as he went, a puff per each of 20 cigarettes.

Bob Jones, whose body was an aging and slowly-eroding temple, of course did not inhale.

He rubbed a ball of wadded-up toilet paper in the grease.

And heard shuffling and slamming noises.

Directly overhead.

The slamming ceased. The shuffling moved toward the

stairwell.

Shit!

Bob moved on the balls of his feet and crouched in a cube that gave him a view of the stairs.

The shuffling became thumping.

An old man emerged carrying a glass jar filled to the top with coins. Scruffy in jeans and T-shirt, walking with a bit of a limp, he glanced furtively left and right, then went out a door.

Christ Almighty, the old boy had broken in to steal pocket change. Master criminal that he was, he'd stolen the prize for an upcoming office pool, a monthly drawing.

He looked familiar to Bob too. Wrinkles and a paunch and thin, gray hair erased youth, but the eyes did not lie.

Glen Carter.

It was Glen Carter in the putrid flesh. When had Bob last seen his erstwhile brother-in-law?

Twenty years at the very least. He had been living with Bob and Gwen, sponging off them, claiming he was job hunting, another of his multitude of lies.

Shortly after Laura's birthday party, it was. She was a barely-manageable teen and relatives were in from out-of-town for the party.

The following week, Bob got after Gwen to bug Laura about writing thank-you notes.

Boozing hard, Gwen was still semi-functioning.

Gwen and Laura got into one of their screaming arguments.

Bob stepped in and refereed. As if he didn't have anything else to do, working 80 hours a week, building Jones Armament and Research.

Laura claimed she'd written the thank-yous and had the *complete* list, checking them off as she went.

Father Sir.

Smart-ass kid, but damned if she wasn't right. Eight people who attended weren't on the list. People, Bob knew, who had left envelopes, not wrapped presents. Envelopes containing cash, envelopes the birthday girl never received.

His worthless, thieving douche bag of a brother-in-law! Had to be.

Bob sent Glen out on an errand, giving him time to search his room. In three minutes, he found tens and twenties under his mattress, a brilliant place to hide his loot.

When Glen Carter returned from the errand, Bob threw him out on the spot. His sister had not objected, agreeing that it was the last straw.

Bob Jones went out the same side door and watched Glen Carter climb into a beat-up 1957 Plymouth Fury coupe, so old it had a wraparound windshield and tail fins.

Bob was 56 years of age and looked older. The three years in the can, buggered by Mr. Higgins, the wire fraud scofflaw (Next on his list), had not been kind.

Prison in general, country club or not, was no fountain of youth.

Glen, a year younger than Bob, was *fossilized.*

The Plymouth discharged a rooster tail of blue smoke, easier than easy for Bob to trail in his 1980 Mercedes 450SL that was so new it smelled like a shoe store.

Glen Carter parked across the street from a grungy tavern. Paint peeled on its door and beer signs hung inside flyspecked windows.

Bob Jones parked a block behind Glen.

Glen didn't get out of the car for a good five minutes. When he did, his front pockets were bulging.

Ninety seconds later, per his gold Rolex that was worth 100 '57 Plymouth Furys, Bob walked to Glen's beater and saw what he expected to see. The hyper-pathetic loser had sorted the stolen coins, gleaning dimes, quarters and half-dollars. Pennies and nickels were scattered on the front seat and floor.

The tavern stank of stale beer and of restrooms not regularly cleaned. Glen was sitting at the bar. A table of geezers playing cards completed the dive's quorum.

Bob took a seat on a wobbly stool two away from Glen.

Glen, who was already starting on his second schooner of draft beer.

Last of the big spenders, Bob's lately brother-in-law protected $25 or $30 in stolen change on the bar between his beer and himself.

Fearing sanitation practices, Bob ordered a bottle of beer. No glass, thank you.

Glen chugalugged his beer, raised the dead soldier, and lit a cigarette.

Must have a hole in it, he told the barkeep, who forced a smile, having heard that one no more than 10,000 times. The bartender giving him his "Oh boy, I'll be able to retire to Tahiti on your tip" look.

Impatiently, Bob stared forward at nothing until the bartender moved on to the geezer table and Glen took a long, thirsty gulp.

Turning, Bob said, hot enough for you?

It's that time of the year, Glen Carter said. Can't escape it.

Glen, do you also despise the air that your sister Gwen breathes?

Huh?

Glen, careful. Don't topple off your barstool. You haven't a parachute on, you know. Glen, did you hear me?

Glen looked at him.

Cat got your tongue, Glen? Cat as in catatonic. Know who's talking to you?

Uh.

Huh and uh. That's articulate of you and you're absolutely right. Bob Jones, Glen. A pleasure to see you after all these years.

Don't want to shake hands? No problem, Glen. A business meeting is what we're having, not a joyful family reunion. Us letting bygones be bygones, yes? On the agenda was what you were *actually* searching for at Free Wil. The metal money, all $40 or $50, was a windfall, not the mission that brought you there.

No comment? Stalling to think up a tall tale? Don't bullshit me. You can't bullshit a bullshitter, Glen. That is a fundamental law of nature. Got your attention, eh? Let's move to a table for a little privacy, shall we?

Bartender, keep the gentleman's glass topped off, please. It does indeed have a hole in it. The check to me too, sir. His money is no good here.

The bartender gave Bob a "It's-your-money, pal" shrug and drew another.

At the table, Bob hoisted his glass.

Cheers, Glen.

With a basset-hound expression Glen hoisted his, but did not clink. He looked at his glass and took a big swig of suds.

The mission, Glen. Your mission. The reason you're treating our fair city with your presence after all these years. Speak if you wish the free beer to flow.

Free beer to flow were the magic words.

Thus came a logorrheic spewing.

How Glen went to his old man's house. Key didn't work. No surprise that the old man changed the locks. Tight as we were, the senile old fucker, he went and changed the locks on me all the time. Walked around the house, looked in windows. Must of changed furniture and stuff too. It's been awhile, but ain't none of it there. Then this guy come out, young guy, a prick in a suit and tie, asking what's going on, me telling him it's the old man's house, me asking what *he* was doing there, him saying he was the owner on account of it being sold off by the daughter of Mr. Elmer Carter who went and died, me saying nobody told me and she's my sister, Mr. Carter's daughter. Him, this guy, the motherfucker, he went and laughed in my face and looked me up and down, saying an important person like Gwen Carter, having a brother like me, no way, giving me 60 seconds to get my ass off his property or he'd call the fucking cops. Yeah, so why's she so important? He said don't you read the paper? Gwen Carter and Laura Wilson, two gals running Free Wil, a computer outfit growing by leaps and bounds, so that's how come you saw me in that place of theirs, seeing if they're on paper side by side, you know. Gwen owes me half on the old man's house. Me, who ain't got a pot to piss in or a window to throw it out of. That and being what you'd call you're disabled on account of an injury to both feet around five years ago when some rotten motherfuckers rolled me and stole my shoes, me having to walk on nasty pavement and shit in the dark, cutting 'em and falling down till a ambulance went and come for me. That's the law, ain't it? She gotta share half? Right?

Absolutely right, Glen. How unfair. How grossly unfair of her. You're off seeing the world, Glen, that's no reason to steal your inheritance. You could go to court if you have money to pay a lawyer, but there's another way.

Yeah? What other way?

One that requires patience by yourself.

How much patience?

Okay, Bob said, let's say that Gwen invested a large chunk or all of the proceeds of the house sale into Laura's company, seed money to move it out of the garage, Gwen's or Laura's garage, where all start-ups seem to start up.

Conceivably, you could be equal partners.

The mental math was easy, Bob didn't say. If the sale of her father's house, *their* father's house, financed Free Wil, Inc., her brother, dissolute as he was, was entitled to half, therefore, theoretically making him a 25% shareholder in Free Wil.

Naturally they'd fight it, he thought. An obligation connected to half the sale's proceeds was a reach. The father may've written his loser of an offspring out of the will too and who could blame him.

Let's say, Glen Free Carter hired a greedy lawyer, an oxymoron and redundancy. Hired him on a contingency to sink his fangs into Gwen, who knows how Glen and Bob might fare? To be sure, they'd be on shaky legal ground, but there was a chance Glen might win and they'd be reluctant to assume that risk.

And buy him off. To be rid of him. For a hefty pile of *dinero*.

Give it a year, he decided. Bob Jones had the Swiss bank and offshore cash to tread water. Let Free Wil keep growing like a weed. Them going public wasn't impossible either.

The *dinero* pile from a molehill to a mountain? Maybe. Providing him ample time to have some fun with Mr. Higgins.

Glen, incidentally, did you find anything of interest at Free Wil?

Shrugging, he said, can't tell. Some old papers, lots of them, with "Laura Jones Wilson and Gwen Jones Carter dba" on them. What's this dee-bee-eh mean?

Doing Business As. Which confirmed that the two women were financially joined at the hip. Glen had accidentally done excellent work, him and his idiotic covert operation.

Dba is a misspelling of "dab", Glen. An incompetent typist transposed the letters.

Glen said he thought it's something like that. But what's dab mean?

Dab is business slang for "dabble", meaning they dabble or touch different aspects of the business.

Oh.

Anyway, Glen, a proposition for you. Allow me to subsidize you for one year. One year to the day. Apartment, food and beer money, gasoline for your classic car. Then we get what you're owed. Trust me. Patience. It'll be worth the wait.

Yeah? What's in this for you, Bob?

Half.

Half?

Fifty-fifty. Half of a small fortune. What say, partner?

How come a year?

Their company's growing by leaps and bounds. We'll ride that bandwagon and make even bigger bucks.

Glen frowned, thinking. He asked how much beer money?

Bob Jones smiled, spreading his arms. How much beer can you drink? That's how much beer money. Beer that'd fill a swimming pool.

Glen Carter shook his hand.

HUBERTICIUM. *A highly-radioactive synthetic element with the periodic-table symbol Hu. Half life of approximately 34.761 seconds. Atomic weight: 262. Atomic number: 104. Physical characteristics: appearance unknown, but believed to be a silver-grey metal. Discovered and first synthesized in 1969 by Dr. H. H. Hubert. Uses: None known.*

Obsessed with developing practical applications for huberticium such as thermonuclear warfare, Dr. Hubert devoted his life to isolating the element and stabilizing it in a compound. World War III would eventually be upon us, so we might as well win it. World War IV too.

It will never be determined if Dr. Hubert achieved his goal of creating huberticium trichloride ($HuCl^3$). On Wednesday August 12, 1981, radiation alarms sounded throughout the building that housed his laboratory, the source of the contamination quickly traced to him.

The building and adjacent buildings were evacuated. Thankfully, no personnel suffered radiation exposure.

No one but Dr. Hubert.

Four men in hazardous materials garb went in for him.

At the sight of Dr. H. H. Hubert, all four lost their lunches.

On Thursday, August 13, 1981, Bob Jones sat waiting in a junk food restaurant. He was going to surprise an old colleague, the restaurant manager. He was expected momentarily, after a doctor's appointment. Bob had asked the hired help to inform the manager that Bob wished to have a word with him on an extremely urgent matter.

Then he'd drop in on Glen Carter. It had been a year to

the day since their handshake.

A busy, busy day for Bob Jones.

He was *so* thrilled!

He passed the time with the morning paper.

There was an interesting front-page story. A mad scientist and his radioactive love child, an artificial element he'd invented named huberticium, had had a fatal falling out.

Huberticium was radioactive to the extreme. A four-block area was sealed off until the radiation danger was evaluated.

There were no casualties except for the mad scientist, Dr. Hubert H. Hubert, 61.

Elementally coincidental, Bob Jones thought.

Dr. Hubert had his huberticium problems.

The restaurant manager, courtesy of Bob Jones, had his problems with an element listed earlier in the periodic table:

LEAD. *A soft, malleable metal with the symbol Pb, Atomic number 82; Atomic weight 207.2. Specific gravity 11.35. Physical characteristics: Dull silvery-gray. History: In common use for thousands of years. Current Uses: Bullets, lead-acid batteries, solder, weights. Former uses (discontinued due to toxicity): Tetraethyl gasoline to reduce engine knock, children's toys, pigment in artists' paints*

A man leaning on a cane made his way from a rear door to the front counter. A young woman at the cash register nodded at Bob as she spoke.

Bob got up when the man slowly approached, saying that it appeared to be busy in his fine restaurant and that he wouldn't take much of the man's valuable time and to please have a seat.

The man sat. He was trembling.

Taking a job here and working your way up to manager. Kudos, sir. No way can an ex-con reenter his old profession as a bond trader, is there? You gotta do what you gotta do. This is a prime job for a pedophile too, parents bringing the little ones in all day long to eat this garbage you sell that the rug rats love. It must be frustrating. You can ogle but not touch. Kind of like a red-blooded male eyeballing pretty girls in skimpy clothes.

Blank stare.

You don't recognize me, do you, Mr. Higgins? And forgive me for saying it's vice versa. You are a shadow of the Mr. Higgins who I feared and detested in our country club dormitory.

Mr. Higgins didn't reply.

One of the symptoms of long-term lead poisoning is memory loss and the inability to concentrate. Ticking them off on his fingers, Bob went on. Stomach cramps, vomiting, fatigue, headaches, muscular weakness.

If your doctor hasn't diagnosed lead poisoning, you should be in the market for another doc — no, forget that. It's far too late. It'd be a waste of money needed for funeral expenses.

Don't recognize me, Mr. Higgins?

Blank stare. Trembling lips.

No?

You know how to hurt a bitch's feelings, don't you?

Moving right along, Mr. Higgins, how do you suppose you contracted lead poisoning? Let's say that a person knows a person, an oddball in the computer profession to whom he introduced a young lady who hauled his ashes. The second person had mentioned in passing to the first person that an uncle of his, an antique hippie, was a failed artist, a painter who kept at it when he was of a mind to and when he had a functioning mind. The bohemian was a walking pharmacy of controlled substances. He'd sampled them all.

The first person had been researching methods of inflicting a slow, painful death and getting away with it. Well, the information-gathering took him to good, old untraceable lead. Lead that used to be in artist pigment, before the anti-lead crusades. Unleaded gasoline and so forth.

Artists swear that lead white paint, aka flake white, is superior to its replacement, titanium white. A whiter white. Tubes of flake white were given to the first person. No questions asked by the second person.

Your apartment was easy to enter and your refrigerator was my canvas. Yours truly, the artist, is no Michelangelo and your digs isn't the Sistine Chapel.

Two tubes of flake white were utilized in any number of foods. It's amazing how much white stuff we consume. You're a big milk drinker, so that one was the easiest. A spoonful per half gallon, shaken well.

If you had longer to live, you should consider investing in a deadbolt. If for no other reason, those pictures you keep of little boys. Stroke photos from your viewpoint. Tsk tsk.

It is a shame that you must come to work every day. If you didn't, your employees will steal you blind.

Bob looked at his gold Rolex. Listen, it's time to run along. Busy day. Gotta scoot.

You're a busy man. As far as your condition is concerned, there's good news and there's bad news. The bad news is that your symptoms will worsen. The good news is that your suffering will be over soon. One morning you won't wake up.

Two to three months is my unprofessional ballpark guess. Your suffering will come to an end, surrounded by loved ones.

If you had loved ones, Mr. Higgins.

Bob Jones rose to his feet and told Mr. Higgins to have a nice day. As today was the first day in the rest of his life.

Mr. Higgins tried to spring to his feet to commit an act of homicide.

He could not.

≈≈≈

Bob Jones didn't bother knocking on Glen Carter's front door. He had a key and Glen either had the TV on or was napping.

He was doing both, curled up on the couch.

A soap opera. You've lowered yourself even further, Bob said, shutting the television off.

What's tonight? Thursday, it is.

From the coffee table, Bob picked up a TV schedule that was surrounded by empty beer cans and the putrefied remains of TV dinners.

The Waltons and *Magnum, P.I.* A goulash of wholesome and macho. They're summer reruns, but you wouldn't remember, he told the half-awake Glen.

Glen Carter sat up and scratched. His gut had doubled

in volume in one year. Bob Jones pictured himself managing a feedlot occupied by one steer, pacified and fattened for slaughter.

For a last stroll in a chute, not fattened by troughs of corn, but a steady delivery of frozen dinners and cold beer.

Glen ventured out less and less frequently in his 1957 Plymouth Fury on errands like haircuts and shopping for toilet articles. A lost soul on the verge of agoraphobia, he was. A boon for Bob Jones, having a critter disinclined to wander.

Bob Jones removed a legal document and a pen from a soft briefcase. The dump wasn't air-conditioned. It was a blisteringly hot day and it smelled fetid, as did Glen Carter. Bob wanted to be out of there.

Patience paid dividends, Bob said, wiping his brow. Yes, it did.

Yeah?

Oh yes. Yes sir. Your benighted sister fears our alliance and our potential mischief.

Yeah?

With the back of a hand, Bob swept empties and foul-smelling meal trays onto the floor. He opened his papers to the last page, laid them on the table (hoping they didn't stick) and gave Glen the pen. Fifty-one percent of the house sale will be yours.

Free Wil continues to print money. Its value increased 44%. Our attorney says that once you sign, the mouse trap will have snapped shut on this rat of a sister of yours.

Glen squinted at the fine print and said he had a question.

Shit, Bob thought. Oh shit. Shit shit shit.

Yes, Glen?

Next food delivery, can we have them go and bring more of them fried chicken dinners? These Salisbury steak ones, they suck.

Moving the papers closer to Glen Carter, a relieved Bob Jones said, certainly, Glen. It'll be next on my agenda.

Glen yawned, scratched and signed.

At the door, Bob called out to him. Glen, have a nice day.

No answer. The television's sound was up.

Oh well, enjoy it while you can, Glen. Bob had stopped food deliveries, effective immediately. The rent was paid to the end of the month.

Bob complied with the terms of the contract by placing a one-dollar bill on a table, George W.'s face up.

Going to his car, Bob smiled, thinking about the terms he'd written.

In payment of the sum of one dollar, the undersigned agrees to the release of any and all claims –

I

INTEGER. *A word for number or digit or figure or numeral or cipher or, obscurely, chiffer.*

On this evening when her estranged father swindled an uncle she hardly remembered and tormented a man he was slowly murdering, Laura Wilson sat out on the patio with Jim and his telescope.

Thursday, August 13, was 1981's hottest day. In fact, the 97° high set a record for August 13. The needle on a thermometer hanging on the outside wall seemed glued at 80.

Quyen was in bed. Her window and door were open. A fan blew in the hallway for cross-ventilation.

On cool evenings when Laura and Jim sat and talked about their days, as Jim scanned the heavens, they drank hot tea. Tonight called for cold beer. The bottles were perspiring as much as they were. It was not a dry heat.

Uncomfortably warm or not, tonight was perfect for star gazing. Laura knew there were billions and billions of stars, as many as one trillion.

How many can one see? Too many to count even for one who thinks of numbers as toys.

Streaking comets were distracting too. Comets or UFOs, one or the other.

Laura had had a brief romance with Roman numerals. They were ungainly playthings more suitable for current events.

Like Super Bowl XV played this year: Oakland XXVII, Philadelphia X.

Like this year itself: MCMLXXXI. Like today's record-high temperature: XCVII.

Once upon a time, she had a fling with an abacus. She requested and received an abacus on her 10th birthday, a gift from her puzzled parents. The entranced child played with her abacus for years until the onset of puberty shifted her attention elsewhere.

A beautiful instrument of wood and beads and brass corners, it still held sway on her bookshelf. Two beads above a separating bar counting as five, five below counting as one.

The world's first calculator, but too slow, too limited for Laura, the adult.

A work of art retired as ornamentation.

She continued looking up. Billions and billions of stars conjured factorials, which were positive numbers expressed by *n!*

For instance:

1! = 1 x 1 = 1

2! = 1 x 2 = 2

3! = 1 x 2 x 3 = 6

4! = 1 x 2 x 3 x 4 = 24

5! = 1 x 2 x 3 x 4 x 5 = 120

The extrapolated bulk of factorials lent themselves well to the vastness above. She hadn't an inkling what practical use factorials were, but they were fun.

As she moved on from 5!, she observed that Jim was not observing a star, but The Evening Star – Venus, the brightest spot in the sky.

At 9! (362,880), she paused. A trillion stars! What factorial was one trillion?

Laura Wilson went on — 10! (3,628,800)

If she was going to hit that trillion, she'd need a refill of coolant. Inside she went for a cold one.

Jim stubbornly refused to admit eyestrain when his single eye was zeroed in on Venus, but she wasn't fooled.

When he started looking away and blinking, she'd make him stop hunting for Venusian moons. Like tonight.

She patted the step.

He sat.

They'd do a little necking. Then she'd ask him if ought to check if Naugahyde was cooler than the patio.

As they had different coefficients of heat.

He'd nod and say it'd be worth checking out.

In the name of science.

INTERCEPTOR EXTRAORDINAIRE. *That's how Ocean Robert Benson thought of himself, although he did not dare say so. It'd be too cocky. They'd be on his case, all over his ass, making all the contact they could without drawing a yellow or red card.*

Razzing him right off the field.

But that's what he was.

Like now.

Seeing the ball come forward, three players in green shirts, the opposition in this tournament final.

The enemy.

Out of the corner of an eye: the linesman's flag was down.

Nobody was offside.

A clean breakaway.

Four minutes left, the enemy in front, 5-4. Ocean was in white. Other white shirts had pressed forward to score the equalizer, but somebody coughed up the ball.

Nobody was back but Ocean and the keeper. Coaches and teammates were confident that Ocean and the goalkeeper could cover.

Ocean Benson was *that* good.

Bastard child that he was. Sired by a rat turd, his mother said. But no less perfect for it.

It was a cloudy Saturday, May 22, 1982. Thunder-showers were predicted for later. Nervous coaches and parents glanced at the dishwater-gray sky.

Ocean didn't care.

He'd play with lightning crackling around him.

He'd play in a blizzard.

He'd play in a dust storm.

He'd play in a hurricane.

He'd play in a hailstorm, hail the size of golf balls plummeting out of the sky.

He'd play if it were 200° degrees or -200°.

The Toms, Dicks and Harrys who used to tease Ocean for his name no longer did. They envied and admired his skill and toughness.

Ocean Benson's position was fullback or central defender. In kid soccer, players tended to ignore coaching when under stress, moving hither and yon, as if a herd of cats.

Ocean was a self-proclaimed sweeper. He did not stray past midfield.

Everybody else on the field in this or any other match wanted to put the ball in the net. They dreamed of it.

Ocean Benson dreamed of intercepting the ball, of keeping the ball out of *his* net.

Ocean, a 12-year-old, whose height and weight were in the median, could kick a soccer ball 35 yards.

He dared them to advance the ball into territory he *owned.*

He double-dared them.

He daydreamed of growing up and playing at the highest professional level. He'd go by one name like the best Brazilians.

Oscar, Zico, Júnior, and the greatest ever, Pelé.

Ocean.

Ocean had a theory that the world's greatest athletes like Pelé could see half a second into the future. How else do you explain how they deflected an enemy ball they couldn't possibly see or make that pass to an attacker through so much traffic?

Here they came, three green shirts to one white — him. The team in green was disciplined and skilled and well-coached. They wouldn't be in the tournament final if they weren't.

Ocean Robert Benson, interceptor extraordinaire, drifted into the penalty area, mindful of not blocking his keeper's view of the ball.

He lived for this, for mismatches.

Commit yourselves. Make your move!

Which the enemy winger to Ocean's left did. He sent the ball across to the second enemy in the penalty area. The third enemy was running at the opposite goalpost, ready to flick a pass or a rebound into the net.

An easy goal.

Not if Ocean Benson had anything to say about it.

He took the ball in the air, heading it harmlessly to the left, to deny the winger a shot on goal. The enemy winger tried to center it to the third enemy, who moved toward the penalty spot. But not fast enough. Ocean sent a hard side volley at the enemy winger. The ball ricocheted against him and over the back line.

Goal kick for the white team.

Demoralized, deflated, frustrated, pissed off, their easy goal thwarted, the greens retreated as the keeper rolled the ball to Ocean, whose booming kick sent the ball on to a *white* mismatch at the green goal.

The whites smelled blood. No organization here, just blast the ball when it came to them.

And blast the ball again.

And again.

It pinballed off the enemy keeper's hands, off players, off the iron.

Then in, plumping the back of the net.

Goal!

Five-five now. Two minutes remained.

Jim Wilson was on his feet. Venus was going to be low in the sky, in the direction of and not much higher than the top of the green's net. His full attention should've been on the game. He shouldn't have been distracted by the heavens he could not see, but he couldn't help himself.

Not as long as Venus held more secrets.

Quyen Wilson, beside him, was on her feet, yelling and cheering louder than anybody for Ocean and his team.

Mary Ann Benson was on her feet. Ocean and BREAD were her life, in that order.

Why name me Ocean, he'd asked her? Because that's the depth and breadth of your beauty and talent and goodness.

She stayed on her feet as Ocean, who had gone forward, took the ball away from a green player at midfield, booted it all the way to the enemy penalty area and a teammate, and—

Goal!

Six to five, white team.

Less than one minute remained.

Ocean stood back in his penalty area, hands on hips.

His penalty area.

Her beloved son's private real estate, Mary Ann thought.

At long last, she had a good man in her life.

One-night stands with men whose names she had

forgotten didn't count. They were entertainment.

When she thought of Ocean in that context, she wondered very, very briefly what had happened to the two bad men in her life.

≈≈≈

One bad man in Mary Ann's life, Roscoe Snails, was not on his feet at the soccer match. He'd simply vanished. Not a great surprise, him (she theorized) in the employ of some ultra-sneaky spook agency, just his speed.

Had Roscoe – what was that stupid spy movie expression? – gone to ground? Maybe he was snapping pictures of air bases in Algeria or from a submarine off Red China.

Not that she gave a damn. She was mildly curious.

≈≈≈

The second bad man in her life, Bob Jones, biological father of Ocean, was not on his feet at the soccer match. The rat turd transcended bad. Even *evil* didn't do him injustice.

Mary Ann had not seen him nor heard of him of late, but she *felt* him.

≈≈≈

Gwen Carter was not on her feet.

Laura Wilson was not on her feet.

Gwen and Laura couldn't be at the soccer match.

They had no choice but to miss it. They were spending their Saturday in Free Wil, Inc.'s boardroom with their attorneys. All were in agreement that Bob Jones' lawsuit was frivolous. Glen Carter, whereabouts unknown, had signed over his rights to 50% of Elmer Free Carter's estate to Bob Jones.

It'd be helpful to know what was going through Glen Carter's pickled brain when Bob Jones glommed onto him and conned him into signing that paper. Glen, who was, at that exact moment, *somewhere* enjoying a drink of fortified wine in a paper bag. Most of the time, Glen couldn't tell you where he was if you asked him.

That Jones was owed half was not in dispute. His contention that he was therefore an equal shareholder in Free Wil, Inc. was. Yes, the importance of Gwen's investment in Free Wil's financial health was indisputable, but the ownership connection was tenuous.

Best to settle with Jones, the lawyers advised. If he'd settle. You couldn't predict what went through the minds of jurors.

Laura thought of the comedian who performed at the company picnic two years ago. Buster something. His last name wasn't memorable, but his bit on lawyers was.

Pay the monster what it'd take? Gwen and Laura had a big problem with that. No settling with the monster.

Then we'll have to prepare for the worst, the lawyers said.

The suit was on the docket for Monday morning.

So prepare for the worst is what they did Saturday and Sunday too, them and their lawyers.

The Wilson twins were not on their feet. They were at Free Wil, Inc. too, working from a list given by Laura as the boardroom powwow went on, hunting any and all files the attorneys thought might be required.

Richard Wilson missed his wife terribly. He missed her every minute he was apart from her, if only for the weekend on the job.

David Wilson Junior missed her too because he wanted to throw up every one of the million times his brother told him he missed his wife.

David, who hung out with the boys, drank beer, and picked up girls in bars. He knew a slut when he saw one.

The twins were less impossible to tell apart. They were gradually going their separate ways. They didn't dress identically and their interests were varying. This was mostly David's doing, so disgusted was he by Richard's choice of mate and what she was doing to him.

≈≈≈

Kelli Wilson, recent bride of Richard – lavish church wedding, white dress that cost as much as a Buick Riviera, honeymoon in St. Tropez, the whole shebang – was not on her feet at the soccer match or anywhere else.

She was on her knees, her basket of blonde tresses bobbing.

It bears repeating that Bob Jones was not on his feet. He was not at the soccer match at which his biological spawn starred. He would not have been there even if he did not steadfastly deny paternity. He had no time for kids or anything else that did not center on Bob Jones.

Naked from the waist down, he lay on the bed in his suite as Kelli did her magic.

Kelli, who would not put out for the dirty old man. She refused in not so many words. Like, *hello*, wasn't it obvious?

Jones was, like, so gross. As gross as the dirty old men she'd known as a child, family friends and relatives. She learned early on to sit on their laps if they held out their arms to her. If she squirmed a little, just the right way, she'd feel their weewees growing underneath her bummy.

For this, she knew there'd be a second dessert or change for her piggy bank.

Kelli had gone down on guys since she was 15-years-old. She lived with her divorced mother who was a cocktail waitress. Her mother didn't always come home at night, so Kelli was on her own to date who she liked, whenever she liked.

If her mother had been drinking a lot, she'd bring the guys home with her. The wall separating Kelli and her mother's bedrooms was tissue-thin. Kelli stuffed tissues in her ears so she couldn't hear the noises from the other side of the wall.

So she could sleep.

It wasn't the same as doing the big nasty, which girls Kelli knew did to be popular, but it was plenty bad enough. Kelli didn't like to go down on guys, so she'd think about other stuff while she was, important stuff like her upcoming hair appointment or the kind of the car the boy she was going down on had, until he finished.

Kelli had never liked being touched but she had always liked making guys ache to touch her, licking their lips and fidgeting and squirming as they did. She learned fast to prick-tease them beforehand so they'd finish quick.

After they finished, it was a long time until they wanted to touch her again.

A preacher she'd once gone down on (after he gave her money for a nice dress to wear at Sunday school, which she never attended) lectured her (afterward, not before) on how the Bible said sodomy was a sin.

Kelli-who-dotted-the-i-with-a bubble Wilson hadn't

read the Bible, but knew the preacher was lying. If he could tell his wife he was leading a prayer meeting instead of being blown by her, he was a liar plain and simple.

Besides, sodomy had to do with horses and sheep, not what she was doing.

Didn't it?

Bob Jones wasn't offended at her making a face when he'd propositioned her. She was well paid for another service she performed for him and was now earning her bonus.

Bob was in a rare good mood too for several reasons:

He was not going to show in court on Monday.

Let them have a default judgment as their shysters bleed them dry, umpteen bucks per hour.

He didn't need the money a favorable judgment would garner.

Free Wil Inc. wasn't long for the world. It'll be worthless, rendering 2. and 3. inapplicable.

J

J-ALPHA. *Advanced state-of-the-art, next-generation, cutting-edge Free Wil, Inc. home computer. Scheduled for release on March 30, 1984. Specifications: formerly top secret; presently in the public domain.*

The irony of that date was not lost on Laura Wilson and Gwen Carter as they wrote and signed paychecks for the company's remaining employees. Today was Friday, March 30, 1984.

The last weekday before April Fool's Day.

Neither was in danger of undergoing writer's cramp. The company was down to nine employees.

J-Alpha was here, there and everywhere. Features and technical specifics were in professional journals and, two weeks ago, a general-interest science magazine found at newsstands and in grocery stores. Photos of the prototype and the first production units too.

J-Alpha was in the public domain. Competitors were welcome to borrow or steal.

Laura Wilson thought of the plunder as a technological smorgasbord.

Whoever sold them out had done so thoroughly and mercilessly. J-Alpha was useless on the marketplace and there was no successor to Useless in the works. All research work and money had gone into J-Alpha, an enormous gamble that should have paid off. Would have paid off but for the sellout.

This corporate funeral was not taking place at the Free Wil, Inc. campus.

Even if they'd wanted to turn off the figurative and literal lights there, the campus was unavailable. All locks had been changed.

The campus had gone into voluntary foreclosure. Free Wil, Inc. had filed bankruptcy. It belonged to banks, who auctioned furnishings to cover (unsuccessfully) payments in arrears on first and second mortgages.

As a joke, Gwen said the wrap-up should be a wake, not a funeral, preferably in a fun place like a sports bar. Laura thought it was a terrific idea, but are you going to be okay in a sports, well, bar? Considering the stress and all?

Gwen said that she'd been exposed to temptation for the last 18 years and three months, so not to worry.

She'd even pick the bar and have a table set up for them.

Televisions hung above the main bar and in corners, visible to all. A smattering of drinkers watched a preseason baseball game on TV as they drank beer, smoked cigarettes, and talked sports.

Its back bar held shelves of hard liquor. Indirect lighting caused the liquid in the transparent bottles to glow jewel-like.

Free Wil's table occupied an alcove. At Laura's request, management had muted the baseball game on sets that interfered with their conversation. The checks had been written before the funeral/wake and were in envelopes.

Daisy Allen, granddaughter of a slave and Free Wil's

Director of Housekeeping Services, sat at the table, eyes red. She accepted her check and complimentary words from the partners. She stood and praised her bosses and coworkers and the company, God bless you all.

To get the words out without bawling, Daisy didn't look at anyone. She looked up at a TV and a baseball game in a silly little stadium that had a desert outside its walls. Her late husband, Lord rest his soul, loved baseball as much as football.

Gwen and Laura returned the praise and then some. They worried about Daisy, wishing they could do more. She had to be 65 or 70. Where would she go, what would she do?

Two J-Alpha project engineers were next. Gwen and Laura scrutinized their eyes and every word and every nuance for treachery.

They detected none. Nor had the private detective agency Gwen and Laura hired. They were unable to trace the leaks of proprietary information that gradually found its way into the competition's recent releases. Or to that mass-circulation magazine's latest issue, a slap in the face.

A Vengeful Slap in the Face, Jim thought when he hired another detective agency on his own without telling Laura. Their assignment was to monitor the only person he knew who was that malicious.

To report Bob Jones' comings and goings from his penthouse, and that of his visitors.

Thus far, *nada*.

Jim Wilson, seated beside Laura for support, scrutinized the engineers. He discerned nothing. He had been scrutinizing his wife too. Jim hadn't seen this level of grief since the miscarriage.

Laura concealed it this time from everyone but her husband, who saw it behind her eyes.

The business failure was not an iota as painful to his wife and mother-in-law as the betrayal.

Jim Wilson ached to hurt somebody.

Jim half-listened as an administrative assistant, two hardware assemblers, and the chief of microchip quality control spoke.

The Wilson twins were last. David Junior spoke for Richard too. Richard who had phoned in ill. Not to go into fine detail, Junior said, but he'd been throwing up, you could tell by his voice.

So that was it, for company and diehard employees.

Eight beer mugs and one ginger ale glass were raised.

No toast given, they clinked and drank.

Gwen was the last to leave. She stayed to settle up with the bar manager.

She wrote a check as he brought her a pack of cigarettes and a whiskey sour.

Gwen gave him the check.

She squeezed and twisted the cigarette package, and tossed it over the bar into a wastebasket, then emptied the sour into a sink.

She asked the bartender for a cup of coffee. Black and strong.

He brought it to her and facial tissues for her tears.

The bartender said he'd be there and at his apartment with her as long as she wanted.

To save her from herself, from temptation overcoming her, he didn't say.

JOHN, A DEAR. *A letter associated with members of the Armed Forces serving far away from home, a wife asking for a divorce or a girlfriend breaking an engagement or a less formal romantic relationship.*

Some GIs were superstitious about having a tattoo done, the personally binding tattoos, such as a heart and arrow, his name and his true love's name within.

They'd heard horror stories of guys who were in a tattooist's chair having it done as their ladies, however many time zones they were apart, simultaneously deposited a Dear John into a mailbox.

If they didn't get the tattoo removed or tattooed over, their future dating pool was damned until death did them part, restricted to females of the same name, even if it was Hester or Lizzie.

Jim and Laura Wilson went home after Free Wil Inc.'s corporate funeral. Laura said she was ready for a nap. By the looks of her — totally wiped out — she did. A long nap.

Jim said that after she slept, he'd have wine cooled and the garage heater on, to remove the chill from Impala's Naugahyde.

She smiled, a *real* unforced smile, and said it was a date.

Jim sat in the dining room with a beer and looked out where the swing set used to be. Quyen was too old for it now. Quyen who was at Mary Ann's for the day.

Jim Wilson ran the warehouse at BREAD and filled in at the office. He made special pick-ups and deliveries too.

Demand increased, increasing the demand for increased supply, he'd say, fishing for a chuckle and a donation.

Jim had plenty to do. But what of Laura? All she had plenty of now was time. Time to stew and to worry about debts outside of what the corporation was liable for.

And to hate who'd done this to Free Wil and many good people.

Jim finished the beer. Before going to the fridge for a second, he checked his answering service.

One call, the operator said. Five minutes ago. From Jim's private eye, who was waiting beside a phone booth at the end of the block from the subject's.

Please call back ASAP.

The detective picked up on the first ring and Jim asked what's up?

He told Jim that Jones hadn't had a visitor in five days who wasn't a deliveryman. Nor had the subject gone out. Who did he think he was, Howard Hughes?

In person, the PI could be mistaken for a CPA.

On the phone a film noir actor.

Please get to it.

Well, this doll went in and up to see him. She knew the front door code and let herself in.

Doll?

Oh yeah a doll! A babe, a dish. Got out of a taxi. Kept the taxi waiting out front. Miniskirt. All-world bazooms. Legs all the way up to her ass. We're talking super-fine quiff.

A blonde?

Yeah.

With big hair?

How'd you know?

Lucky guess.

The PI said he'd hustled to the cabbie, gave him a double sawbuck to tell him where she was going next and to keep his yap shut to her. The hack said airport. Her packed bags were in the trunk.

She's upstairs like 15 minutes. Back in the cab and away she goes.

Jim thanked the private eye for his good work and to please send his final bill.

Which the detective said he would and don't forget the twenty to the cabbie that he doesn't have a receipt for. It'll be on the billing.

Jim Wilson left as quietly as possible, drove to on Richard and Kelli Wilson's apartment, and knocked on the door.

David Junior answered, surprised to see his big brother, whose index finger to his lips.

Jim walked in without invitation, entering an inversion layer of cigarette smoke.

What's the matter with Richard? Flu? Food poisoning?

Worse. Kelli left him.

When?

Yesterday. Read this.

My dearist Richard.

It's not in my nature to be sneeky, but I moved out yesterday while you were at work and packing up to shut down the company so as to not hurt you any furthur. Let me furst say it isn't you, it's me. I didn't tell you before we wed that I don't like being tutched even though I let you do the big nasty sticking your thing in me as much as you wanted when we were dating so you can't blame yourself as it is not you it's me. The other thing I try to do to you,

you say it's not what nice girls do and for that I respeckt you deeply. I'm not good enuff for you, Richard. You're so smart and I'm not. You come home from work and tell me what you have worked on that day. You even show me pictures. You are so payshunt when I ask you dum tecnicull things. So I must say goodby and farewell. It is time we both move on. I will always have a soft spot in my heart for you and love you forever.

My lawyer will be getting in tutch.

Kelli°

Jim reread the semiliterate Dear John.

He closed his eyes, collecting himself.

Jim had not once in his life laid a hand on his kid brothers, even when he babysat for his parents, and had permission to paddle their butts if they misbehaved.

They seldom did. There were times Jim was tempted to paddle their butts for *not* misbehaving like any kid should, punishing them for suspiciously good behavior, for seeming to emulate Wally and Beaver Cleaver of *Leave It To Beaver*.

Jim balled his fists. Where the hell is he?

Fingertip to lips again. The bedroom, trying to sleep.

The bedroom door was locked. Jim kicked the door. Kicked it and kicked it.

Open the fucking door, Richard!

He opened it.

Terrified, Richard's cheeks were caked with dried tears.

Jim smelled urine. He remembered Richard pissing himself as a kid when agitated and frightened.

He blubbered how interested Kelli was in his work.

How impressed she was, how proud of him she was, how eager she was to see what he'd done, how'd he'd bring things home to show her, how'd he tell –

Richard couldn't go on.

Jim clenched his fists. Jim unclenched his fists.

Let He Who Has Never Been Suckered By A Babe-Dish-Doll Cast The First Stone, Jim thought.

He hugged and hugged his kid brother.

Jim vowed to keep it a secret from Laura. Her hating Richard for life wouldn't do either of them any good.

KILLDEER, THE is *not a deer. It is a bird in the plover family. A killdeer's most distinguishing characteristic is its stilt-like legs. From a distance, the killdeer is frequently mistaken for a sandpiper. The adults are eight inches long. They feature a white belly and breast with two black bands, and a brown back and wings.*

Killdeers are foragers that mainly eat insects. They are migratory birds. When they come north in the spring, they breed and nest in pastures, open fields, and lawns.

One lawn selected by a male and female killdeer for a nesting ground was Dave and Brenda Wilson's. On Saturday afternoon, May 4, 1985, Dave discovered that they had company when he pulled the lawnmower out of the storage shed to mow the backyard. The last couple of weeks had been too rainy and damp to cut grass, so the back had gotten ankle-high.

As Dave bent to pull the starter cord, he saw movement behind the vegetable garden. He tiptoed through the garden until he saw the nest. It was flattened grass with four black-and-white speckled eggs that looked like stones.

Dave went inside and told Brenda, who was cutting up potatoes and carrots for a pot roast. They watched out the kitchen window.

By and by, a bird landed at the nest and sat on the eggs.

The Wilsons didn't have a bird book, so Brenda ran across the street to knock on a neighbor's door. A retired couple lived there. They had bird feeders in their back yard. Brenda knew they went on birding walks too.

Brenda asked them over. They came with binoculars and a field guide. It wasn't long until another bird landed. The birders were of a consensus that the visitors were killdeer.

What do we do, Dave asked?

A little tall grass doesn't hurt anybody, the retired wife said.

The lady who raised holy heck if anybody on the block let dandelions get out of hand, Brenda thought.

As the killdeers nested, neighbors the retirees knew came by to see. They brought neighbors the Wilsons hadn't known. Neighbors brought neighbors the Wilsons hadn't known either.

Brenda kept a coffee pot on and freshly-baked cookies on the counter.

By the time the chicks hatched and grew, and the killdeer family was gone, the back half of the yard was knee high. The Wilsons, who hadn't known anyone outside of their immediate neighborhood, now knew folks two blocks away.

Dave got after the grass with a sickle and his mower, believing the effort and the mess was well worth it.

KOSMIK KALAMITATION. *February 2, 1986. Elmer Carter will have been gone 10 years on July 4*th*, but Gwen Carter was not done going through his papers.*

Photo albums and the shoeboxes were stacked to the ceiling against one wall in the hot water heater room off the garage in the townhouse Gwen shared with Mary Ann Benson and Ocean Robert Benson. The room smelled of chlorine and nostalgia.

It was a combination of the sheer bulk of documents and painful memories of his passing that left this chore unfinished.

For the most part, the boxes contained his theories and calculations and his explanatory notes, such as they were. The best she could determine, they were in no particular order, nor did they fit a pattern.

When a light bulb went on in his head, he'd write his brainstorm down.

Some were even wilder than his Carter's Gaps. Like the one she came upon today:

$$\frac{\Delta y}{\Delta x}\frac{xy}{dx}e^{-ti\theta}\frac{-b\pm\sqrt{b^2-4ac}}{2a}\sum_f^x 2 = KK \lim_{n\to\infty}\left(1+\frac{1}{n}\right)^n + \sqrt[3]{99}$$

$$+ \cos 2 \div e^{-ti\theta}\sqrt{a^2+b^2}\,tan^{-1} f \max_{0\le x\le 1} xe^{-x^2} = \boldsymbol{KK}$$

In a size-9AA box: a sheet of yellow-lined paper folded in quarters with the above formula.

Her Dad had neatly printed Kosmik Kalamination formula on the paper.

KK stood for Kosmik Kalamination, she presumed. Whenever she read her father's goofy wording and spelling, she heard his voice, him explaining to her how it made perfect sense.

Gwen paged through a dictionary before reading her father's scribbled notes. Suspicion confirmed.

The words kosmik and kalamitation existed only in her beloved late father's head.

Gwen Carter did not take the words or the formula lightly or in ridicule. They were, after all, the brainchildren of Elmer Free Carter.

A man who had been a retired chemist, forever itching to contribute in his unique way.

A man who had, among many other laudable accomplishments, freed the planet of a particle of evil, a vicious neo-Nazi by the name of Adrian Newt.

Her father's notes analyzed the abracadabra formula, element by element, from start to ***KK***.

To Dad and Dad alone, it logically followed in his narrative that an unwanted family event will occur on or near a minor holiday at least once to every family.

Gwen went inside and looked at the kitchen calendar.

She thought so; today was Groundhog Day.

She smiled at the coincidence.

How silly, she thought.

The phone rang.

Gwen answered and listened.

No, she said! When?

After the reply, trembling, she hung up.

Mary Ann was working at BREAD.

Ocean was in class.

Gwen hurriedly threw on a coat and stepped into her shoes. She headed to BREAD to break the news to Mary Ann in person.

≈≈≈

Ocean Benson, a sophomore in high school, sat in plane geometry class, kind of watching the blackboard and listening to the teacher, who was lecturing about angles as he drew them with chalk.

Acute, obtuse, right, complementary and vertical angles. Angles that he designated with A, B, C, D, E, F, et cetera.

Ocean visualized the letters as his soccer enemies, attacking players, wingers coming at him from every angle, shooting and passing to teammates in the penalty area.

Vectors and intersecting points and space.

Anywhere but in *his* net.

Ocean visualized curves and parabolas too. How skilled attackers bent the ball.

He doodled: ( ) ≠ ٣ک/┐ ♯ ^

He visualized Quyen Wilson too, as he increasingly did.

Quyen, who would never know who her parents were, nor their fate.

She was incurious, so she said. Some things were better not known, she felt.

He didn't disagree.

Quyen was two doors down in a senior honors zoology class. She was on her way to college with a 4.0 GPA and a full-ride scholarship, med school her eventual goal.

She'll be a great doctor, Ocean knew.

≈≈≈

Daisy Allen was the day's event, a tragic, tragic event. Daisy wasn't a member of the family, but she *was* family.

Her sister, with whom Daisy lived since her husband's death, had phoned Gwen Carter in tears, giving her the tragic news.

Daisy was late for breakfast this morning. Her sister knocked on Daisy's bedroom door. No answer.

The medics who came pronounced her dead. She'd died in her sleep, probably the result of a stroke.

≈≈≈

At BREAD, Mary Ann and Gwen wept, hugging each other. Gwen remembered the family event predicted in KK. This, on or near Groundhog Day.

Could Gwen's eccentric father, him and his goofball formulae have known? Even from the grave?

She wouldn't put it past him.

≈≈≈

The funeral was four days later, on an uncommonly warm February afternoon. The low winter sun was out and the cemetery lawn was squishy from overwatering.

The service was in an open-air tent. A glossy wooden coffin rested at the bottom of a perfectly-rectilinear hole. Thirteen of the 57 in attendance wondered how they did that.

Fifty-four out of the 57 in attendance wondered why doing business with a funeral parlor was the same as doing business at a used car lot.

Roughly half of the 57 were black, friends and family of Daisy's. Gwen had met and personally knew a quarter. She wished she'd known more.

Gwen Carter wished she'd known Daisy Allen better.

The minister was young and black and pleasant, with short hair and a Richard Nixon ensemble of dark blue suit, white shirt and dark tie. He kept the religious angle in the background and told homilies about Daisy and her kind, caring life. How she'd do anything for you.

To forestall losing it, Gwen Carter let her mind wander to others present, the ones she knew well. To them and their ages, her subtraction posting their birthdays later in the year.

Cliché or no cliché, the death of a loved one *did* cause a person to ponder his or her own mortality.

Beginning with herself, Gwen Carter, going on 62. Last year, the big six-oh, had been a trauma.

Making it additionally traumatic was her final visit to The Bar. The bartender wasn't on duty. His replacement said he was on his honeymoon in Maui.

From now on, age will merely be a number to Gwen Carter.

Jim Wilson, 39. The big four-oh upcoming. By all appearances, he was as content as he'd been since before Vietnam.

Laura Wilson, 40. From zillionaire on paper to okay job as software developer. Her a tough, tough, tough woman.

Laura, white-knuckling her husband's hand.

Mary Ann Benson, 56. Tears and more tears, comforted on one side by—

Ocean Robert Benson, 15. Best soccer player in his age group in the state, no contest.

And on the other side by—

Quyen Wilson, 17. Beautiful, brilliant. Self-conscious about her new glasses.

Dave and Brenda Wilson, both going on 60. Bless their hearts. They had seemed 60 for ages, models for Grant Wood's *American Gothic*.

David Wilson Junior (Junior by virtue of being 14 minutes older) and Richard Wilson, 30. The big three-oh. The latter and his darting eyes had undisclosed psychological problems written all over him.

Some problems, everyone in the family supposed, were due to the tramp that ran out on Richard.

How many besides Big Brother Jim knew that Richard had been responsible for Free Wil's downfall? Jim promised he'd keep mum. Did Richard believe him or was he paranoid? If he knew, he could sleep at night. Maybe.

David Junior hadn't set the world on fire either after Free Wil, drifting from job to job, to girl to girl.

The twins were engineering grads, professionals in high demand, so what was their problem?

Gwen gave Bob Jones, age 63, nary a thought.

She didn't know he was at the funeral, albeit clandestinely.

He was not a mourner.

Dressed baggily, with shades and a watch cap, he was mistaken for a cemetery laborer, perhaps the one who dug the hole for the casket.

Standing at the corner of a marble mausoleum 75 yards away. Counting the house. His Swiss and offshore accounts were dwindling, as was his patience and self-control.

Finish the project and he could sleep at night.

One to go.

≈≈≈

Glen Carter, 62. Back on the skids since signing the papers for Bob Jones, he'd learned the hard way that his food deliveries and rent had been cut off.

His current neighborhood: a brushy area next to the city's spaghetti junction, a nickname given to a dense freeway confluence in large cities.

As the minister at Daisy Allen's wrapped up the funeral with the obligatory 23rd Psalm, Glen's throat was slashed. He was bleeding to death inside his home, a cardboard box that had originally been the home of a home entertainment center purchased on sale for $799.95.

Reason for the fatal attack: refusal to hand over a half-empty (or half-full in the opinion of the killer) bottle of Tokay and $2.44 in pocket change.

Per Kosmik Kalamination, Glen's Carter's homicide qualified as *the* second event, as it occurred on or near Groundhog Day, even though Glen had chosen not to be in the family.

L

LAW OF DIMINISHING MARGINAL UTILITY. *A big-time economics term that can go on for pages, replete with equations that'd knock Elmer Free Carter for a loop.*

Why not make it simple?

Why not obey Occam's razor, which postulates that the simplest method is usually the best?

A common example of simplicity and what Law of Diminishing Marginal Utility means is a buffet meal.

Let's say you haven't eaten since lunch and you're starving to death and it's a hot Friday evening, August 21, 1987, the year of the Iran-Contra goofiness. It's been hours and hours since you've eaten. To hell with the heat, you're starving.

You go to the buffet. The joint's packed, so you wait in line at the cashier, pay up, and go in, damn lucky to find a table.

You grab a plate, go to the stations, get into the circular chow lines, and load up with your favorites: fried chicken, mashed potatoes and more fried chicken. On a scale of one to 10, you give this plate a perfect 10.

You sit down and clean said plate.

Your hunger somewhat appeased, you get a new plate and repeat the process. The chow's okay, but you're half full, so it's no longer special. You give it a 5.0 on a scale of one to 10.

So there you have it.

We've all experienced the Law of Diminishing Marginal Utility even if we've never heard of it.

The individual referred to in the second person here is Jim Wilson.

Jim and Laura Wilson did go to a buffet on that warm Friday evening.

Following the buffet, they were going to a movie. First-run films out now were unappealing. Newspapers reviewed the picks of the litter. The Wilsons read the reviews and saw no picks in August 1987's litter.

They were going to a funky downtown theatre with an old-timey marquis. They played artsy flicks and golden oldies. Tonight was *Dr. Strangelove, or How I Learned to Stop Worrying and Love the Bomb.*

It was a *date,* a rare event these days.

With Laura's time at the software developer, frantically writing code to keep up with the competition as she had at Free Wil.

And Jim's time at BREAD, filling in wherever and whenever to keep the payroll low, each averaged a 55-hour week.

Bless her heart, Quyen was off to the college of her choice, at an accelerated summer pre-med program leading to the start of her sophomore year.

They had the house to themselves.

After the movie, the back seat of the garaged 1962 Chevrolet Impala SS awaited, the convertible top down.

The cool Naugahyde beckoned.

Jim Wilson got up to have thirds. He thought he was

full, but wasn't certain. In the Law of Diminishing Marginal Utility, if one was not a glutton, this trip would be a 3.3 on a scale of one to 10, even if it did include dessert.

However, if you were at a buffet and paid $4.99, you wanted your money's worth.

When Jim got to the food stations, he was in a chow line in a canvas tent in South Vietnam, between Pleiku and Ban Me Thuot, three klicks from the nearest village.

He wore green fatigues with PFC chevrons sewn on. He carried a stamped aluminum tray.

PFC Wilson was in the mess tent, in line for noon chow.

Where he should have been, where 27 men died and he hadn't.

Instead of in the orderly room tent, typing on his Underwood portable at 30 words per minute.

This day's chow line had no SOS. You always had SOS, didn't you, always at breakfast and sometimes at noon chow too? This *was* the United States Army.

SOS: Shit On a Shingle. Or in polite company, creamed chipped beef on toast or creamed hamburger on toast.

It's easy to make, Jim Wilson told a guy by him in the chow line.

The guy looked at him funny.

He'd go in the kitchen himself and whip up a batch of SOS if he had to, he went on. It was easy. You take hamburger, flour, milk, salt and pepper, and —

Whoomph.

Did you hear that?

The guy shook his head and sidestepped the weirdo with the eye patch and scars.

This *whoomph* was a round discharging from an American-made 81-millimeter mortar.

A mortar was a steel tube that sat on the ground, steadied by steel legs. If one knew what one was doing, the weapon was accurate up to 3000 yards.

To fire, a shell was dropped into the tube. The projectile fell onto a firing pin that ignited the cartridge primer.

And up it went.

Whoomph.

The round weighed approximately seven pounds including stabilizing fins. This particular weapon had either been stolen by the VC or sold to them by a South Vietnamese ally.

Veteran troops who had been in Korea knew what the *whoomph* was.

Incoming, they yelled. Incoming!

Jim Wilson hadn't served in the Korean War, but he knew from painful experience what the *whoomph* was.

Incoming, he yelled!

Incoming!

A big, blubbery, ponytailed, tattooed guy behind him asked Jim what the fuck was the matter with him and could he move it along?

The slob had a bowling-ball gut and wore a filthy biker outfit of T-shirt and leather pants. Definitely out of standard-issue Army uniform. He carried a heaped plate he planned to heap more on.

The biker was impervious to the Law of Diminishing

Marginal Utility.

On a birthday or Christmas, Laura had been given what they called a coffee table book. It was full of photos of famous art, which they obediently kept on their living room coffee table.

One painting that really nailed Jim between the eyeballs was *Guernica* by Pablo Picasso. The painter was outraged by the Fascist bombing of the Basque village of Guernica in 1937 during the Spanish Civil War. Guernica had no military value whatsoever. Picasso's *Guernica* was a gigantic canvas filled with human and animal parts. The slaughter was tactically meaningless.

Thinking of *Guernica*, PFC James Wilson acted fast. *Guernica* was to befall the mess tent when the mortar round and those to follow struck their target.

To save himself and the biker, Jim drove a shoulder into him, sending him sideways and down.

On the way, the biker swung wildly at Jim, calling him a crazy-ass motherfucker.

A fair assessment at that moment.

The biker's tray and its contents went flying and the pair caromed off the dessert display, bringing all manner of chocolate and cheesecake and pie and strudel down with them.

LIKELIHOOD OF COLLATERAL DAMAGE. *Damage inflicted on one who was not the intended target.*

Bob Jones didn't give collateral damage a thought tonight.

The mission was all.

Gwen Jones's termination of life came down to a coin flip.

Heads, Gwen has a fatal accident.

Tails, she commits suicide

One month ago, Monday, November 30, 1987, an old buffalo nickel went spinning in the air, the Indian on one side, the buffalo on the other, no question which was heads, which was tails.

It landed on the living room carpet in Bob's penthouse suite: tails.

He liked the analogy. The buffalo that had approached extinction. The ex-wife who will be extinct.

It'd be funner too, a challenge, more hands-on. Bob Jones gave himself an end-of-the-year deadline. Bob did his best work when he had a deadline, self-imposed or not.

He'd plan and complete the project on that timetable and be able to sleep at night.

New Year's Eve, December 31, 1987.

A dark and stormy night.

Bob Jones cruised by the same three bedroom-one bath rambler his disowned, traitorous daughter, Laura Jones Wilson, and her pencil-necked failure of a husband Jim Wilson had lived in since — when? — the late 1960s.

What a rut those losers were in.

There was a visiting station wagon in the Wilsons'

driveway. Bob went around the block and parked on the next street, in front of a vacant split-level with a hopeful FOR SALE BY OWNER sign staked in the yard.

Jim Wilson had been dinged a little in Vietnam. Big fucking deal, thought Bob Jones, who had not seen military service in World War Two, albeit profiting handsomely from the conflict.

Serving his country in Bob Jones fashion.

Last summer, the one-eyed loser went berserk at a pig-out buffet, thinking he was back in Nam. Went completely apeshit, damaging property and person. They said it took three cops to subdue him, cops he tried to save from a Vietcong mortar attack.

Oh, it must have been a lovely sight. Entertaining as all get out.

They had a name for Wilson's problem. Seems as if they had a name for every malady and misbehavior in this day and age. In his case: Post-Traumatic Stress Disorder (PTSD).

They treated Pencil Neck's PTSD with therapy (Talking to him in a soothing voice?). Wilson went in for it twice a week, the administrators turning shrinks loose on the poor baby.

The rest of the time, the traumatized fellow stuck around the house, with prescribed sedatives available.

All of this paid by some VA or Pentagon agency, our tax dollars at work.

Bob Jones knew this and other things because of a wiretap. It had cost a pretty penny, a deep chunk out of his reserves, but the service was professional and discreet, first-rate. Twice a week, he received an audio tape.

Thrown in for no extra charge was a front-door key.

Listening to the tapes = Intelligence Gathering.

Intelligence Gathering.

Bob Jones loved that term.

During this holiday season, Jim Wilson, age 41, had a houseful of babysitters as he sulked about, recovering from his PTSD/cowardice/lunacy.

The babysitters were:

Bob's objective, former wife and former drunk, Gwen Carter Jones, age 63, her hymen perhaps growing back from disuse.

Daughter Laura Jones Wilson, age 42.

A miscellany of comers and goers.

The women had plotted to coax Little PTSD Jimmy out of the house for the first time since he was brought home after the "incident".

He was becoming agoraphobic they feared, hunkered down by the shame of what he'd done, that despite assurances by the taxpayer-funded headshrinkers.

Aside from running out of time to do what *had* to be done, age was unimportant to Bob Jones, 65.

His health was okay, but not great.

Nor was he getting any younger.

The plot, the mission, the result of Intelligence Gathering, was to be implemented with brains, not brawn.

He checked his gold Rolex, started the car, and drove around the block. The station wagon in the driveway was gone. The objective of that automobile's occupants was successful.

They had dragged Wilson out of the house to party, to enjoy a little bubbly. To welcome in the New Year and a new life for him.

Leaving *Bob's* objective at home.

Gwen Carter didn't want the temptation of free-flowing alcohol. She had to get going on BREAD's books anyhow, posting recent transactions and tallying year's-end balances.

Operating with volunteers and a few paid employees, her guess was that they'd break even for the year. Not wonderful, not horrible.

She'd be at the dining room table with scratch paper, ledgers and calculator, her favorite pop music on the stereo: *ABBA, Foreigner, Air Supply.*

Bob Jones parked in a next-door neighbor's driveway. This nuclear family was Over the Hill, Through the Woods, to Gramma's House They Went. And would be for three days.

Bob's vehicle, an anonymous gray Pontiac with mud subtly caked to the license plates, in darkness obscuring three out of six characters. The car had been stored in his building's garage, its owner in Mexico for the winter.

In a paper grocery bag on the seat beside Bob: surgical gloves, bottle of chloroform, washcloth, a Mason jar of potent whisky sours, tightly-coiled flexible hose.

Envisage the game plan.

Surreptitious entry.

Prompt immobilization of subject.

Subject removed to garage and placed behind wheel of old Chevrolet (massive smog-belching V-8, an automobile manufactured prior to emission controls).

Her fingers curled around her hand, jar of sours (like the old colored mammy made for her) on the passenger seat (after Bob had poured sufficient beverage in subject's mouth to affect breath and blood alcohol content).

Flexible hose inserted in exhaust pipe, other end into car.

Engine started.

No suicide note necessary.

Bob Jones looked around and saw no peeping eyes. He turned off the Pontiac's dome light, snapped on the surgical gloves, got out with his "groceries", crossed lawns, and inserted his key into the Wilsons' front door knob.

≈ ≈ ≈

Jim Wilson stood by his bed, arms folded. His and Laura's bed. Jim was not feeling very good about himself for an additional reason — the aforementioned bed. They may as well have a Victorian board partitioning them.

Laura had been patient, but it wasn't fair to ask her to wait indefinitely.

For that and for him to jettison the self-pity and be a man.

They were excessively polite to each other, also not a good sign.

Her patience might have come to an end tonight. Laura and Gwen and friends had collaborated to get him out of the house tonight for party-hopping.

They weren't counting on a party pooper, him and his lame excuses. He was coming down with the sniffles. He'd be lousy company. And so forth.

Bullshit.

Jim stepped into his shoes, threw on a sweater, and a jacket over it. He knew their first stop. He'd crank up the old Impala and surprise them there after surprising Gwen here with a see-you-later buss on the cheek as she worked or her books in the dining room.

He'd do it for Laura.

He'd do it for himself.

≈≈≈

Bob Jones was panting, sucking wind. He'd gotten limp, unconscious Gwen behind the wheel of the old Chevy, skidding her by her heels into the garage, hard work for a man of a certain age.

Whiskey sour jar in place. Check.

One end of the flex hose in the tailpipe, the other running over her left shoulder. Check.

Ready for a nice, unhealthy dose of carbon monoxide. Check.

But there was one huge snafu.

Jesus H. Fucking Christ, the convertible top was *down*!

The morons, why keep the top down in the dead of winter?

As in the movies, something always cropped up, something always went wrong to best-laid plans.

Filling the entire garage with a lethal amount of exhaust fumes was too risky. It'd take too long. Too large a volume of fresh, clean air to displace.

She'd awaken and escape.

Unacceptable.

How to get the fucking top up and locked? Where the hell was the button or lever? Must be power. Or not.

He'd locate what he had to, then start the engine, hoping he could get the top up and be on his way before he asphyxiated himself too.

≈≈≈

Dressed for a night on the town, Jim Wilson walked out to the dining room, to soft music, to surprise Gwen. Who wasn't there. Her chair was pulled back, one of her BREAD ledgers opened, upside down on the floor.

The Impala started.

What the hell?

Jim walked into his garage. The Impala's convertible top was coming up, Gwen behind the wheel, slumped, eyes closed. Bob Jones stood at the driver's door, holding a small bottle. The garage was smoky.

Jim Wilson stared.

Bob Jones stared, thinking that the likelihood of a third party on the scene was low. Pencil-neck should be gone partying, but he wasn't.

Everything was turning to shit.

A clusterfuck.

And an opportunity.

Bob was staring at collateral damage.

Wilson couldn't be allowed to live and tell his tale.

In fact, he'd be a participant, Bob Jones's *opportunity*.

Bob Jones coughed, his eyes stinging from the car's exhaust.

He held the chloroform bottle, staring at a loon, a pathetic excuse for a man with scars galore and an eye patch.

Knock him out with the chemical, drag him into the car beside her. A double suicide.

Yeah, unzip and peel down their pants for good measure. A lover's leap, as it were. A perverted and tragically-doomed romance, their horrific fate the result of a wacko Vietnam vet going berserk again.

Come here, boy, Bob Jones said, walking slowly to him. We'll walk out of the free fire zone, you and me. Now come along, don't just stand there, meet me halfway. Or it'll be you alone against the Viet Cong.

Jim Wilson was not experiencing the PTSD episode Bob Jones attempted to trigger. He was experiencing anger and desperation.

He did meet his former father-in-law halfway, yelling at the top of his lungs as he came off the step into the garage, kicking the bastard in the chin, knocking him and his bottle flying against the Impala's fender.

Jim, coughing too, reached into the car, shut off the ignition, and hurried to the garage door, wrenching it upward and wide open.

Jim Wilson went for Gwen, brushing by Bob, who was on his hands and knees, gagging. Jim didn't notice him, single-mindedly going for his mother-in-law. He pulled her out of the car, carried her inside, laid her on the couch, ran to the dining room's rotary wall phone, and dialed 911.

≈≈≈

Bob Jones had to stop for an emergency stoplight as an aid wagon accelerated out of a fire station five blocks away. He knew where it was going.

The light changed and Bob kept going. His jaw was killing him. His chest too, this a new sensation. He knew why the jaw hurt, the cowardly bastard and his kick. His chest ached, an ache that wouldn't go away.

He desperately wanted to stop for emergency treatment.

But certain arrest would follow.

On he drove, destination unknown.

M

MÖBIUS STRIP. *Brainchild of German mathematician August F. Möbius (1790-1868). Simply stated, without the interminable mathematical formulae, a Möbius strip can be made of a strip of paper and a piece of tape. Draw a line down the middle of each side of the strip. Twist the paper and tape the ends. The two lines will join, appearing to be just* one *line.*

Twenty-year-old Quyen Wilson was an outstanding college student on scholarship, but like most college students, Quyen was not rolling in dough.

Christmas this year, 1988, fell on a Sunday. On the prior Monday, she hadn't yet thought of what to get everybody. She paged through some of her textbooks, searching for inspiration. A page in an upper-division math book leaped out at her.

The page was in a chapter on anomalous geometric shapes. The illustration of a Möbius strip was vivid and intriguing.

Quyen was home for Christmas break. When her parents were gone on errands, she went into the garage and took materials from her father's workbench drawers and tools hanging on his wall-mounted pegboard: tin snips, super-stick glue, a file, a can of clear spray paint, a scribe, a steel ruler, a hammer, a T square, a sheet-metal hole punch, and scraps of thick-gauge sheet brass.

Her daddy was not a heartfelt tinkerer. He used tools when he had to. The tools and pieces of wood and metal had accumulated over the years.

Quyen carried it all into her room and got to work. On her desk, she made a Möbius strip out of paper as a model. She liked it.

Between then and Christmas Eve, she worked when she could, when the noise wouldn't give her away. She measured and cut the brass into (15) ¾" x 9" strips.

She filed the edges and corners of the metal to eliminate roughness and sharpness.

She scribed centerlines and marked where the holes were to be.

She punched the holes at half-inch intervals, 108 punches (Her right hand ached for a week).

She polished the brass with cleaner her mommy kept under the kitchen sink.

She sprayed the polished metal with the clear-paint spray to prevent tarnishing.

She twisted the strips and glued the ends.

She tied a decorative ribbon and a small card around each Möbius strip.

Quyen's family and closest friends received the Möbius strips.

They flipped out.

They couldn't take their eyes off of the lines of little holes that played tricks on their eyes.

Nobody could remember having a conversation piece so unique.

Christmas was Merry, a good time had by all.

MOSCOW MULE. *The three scientists gathered at the chief scientist's Moscow apartment to decide a matter of great importance and to enjoy rounds of their favorite drink. They had been enjoying little else of late.*

It was Thursday, June 22, 1989, an ominous date.

Operation Barbarossa commenced 48 years earlier on this very day. Barbarossa was the code name for the Nazi invasion of the Soviet Union.

The Nazis were dead and gone, but different perils loomed. The handwriting was on the wall. The Berlin Wall's days were numbered.

The Wall shall be coming down, the chief scientist warned, like the egg man in that Western children's fable, Dumpty Humpty.

Bitterly, the chief scientist drained the last of his drink.

His acolytes did the same.

The chief scientist gathered the cups and refilled them from a pitcher-full he'd prepared.

The chief scientist's politics had not wavered. He was, now and forever, an evangelical Stalinist. General Secretary of the Communist Party of the Soviet Union's Central Committee, Joseph Vissarionovich Stalin, was his idol, his messiah. With all these failures, the war in Afghanistan and Chernobyl, and this recent treachery, Joseph Stalin must be spinning in his grave.

Uncle Joe would know what to do with glasnost and perestroika and insubordination by the Soviet republics. Uncle Joe would wash the scum down the sewer with its own blood.

The three scientists had kept in touch and grown to

like a cocktail named Moscow Mule. Of the recipe variations in the Mule, the threesome favored one part vodka, one part lime juice, and three parts ginger beer. They omitted the customary simple syrup and sprig of mint.

The scientists compensated for those missing ingredients with a heavier dose of vodka, feeling that syrup and mint sprigs were for ladies, not men.

The chief scientist poured his Moscow Mules into copper cups he had bought on the black market.

They toasted and drank. The chief scientist said it was time to decide. Time for procrastination to end.

Yes Comrade, like it or not, capitalism was arriving soon, said one.

The capitalism train is at the station, said the second. When was the last time you ate a tomato grown on a collective farm? When was the last time you wore a pair of shoes or listened to a radio manufactured at a state-owned factory?

The chief scientist nodded. He asked what the definition of capitalism is from our point of view. Now. Seated in this room. Drinking Moscow Mules.

The others awaited his answer to his own question.

The definition of the term in general is essentially the same, he said. To distill the definition to suit us, capitalism is an economic system characterized by private ownership of goods and services that can be priced and sold in a free market.

Sold to the highest bidder, said the first scientist.

The chief scientist smiled and sipped his Moscow Mule.

Please name a good.

Like an eager student, the first piped up: Bounce. c□aчo□.

The truth *about Bounce, the second cried.*

We have the printed data, the tapes, the photographs, the telemetry readings locked away, said the chief scientist. We have had the evidence for 19 years and two months.

Where can we find capitalism? A free market?

Capitalism, said the overly dramatic second scientist, sweeping his empty copper cup.

Where cannot *we find capitalism, Comrades?*

The chief scientist brought the pitcher, refilled the cups, left the pitcher on the table, went to a desk drawer, and took out a small manila envelope.

When in Rome, do as the Romans do, said the chief scientist, as he dumped the contents of the envelope on the table. He said that he had taken the liberty of investing the money they had saved and given him to hold. There was no decision to make, there would be no procrastination.

Further, he had put out feelers on c□aчo□

The other two were not angry that he had taken this liberty. They were relieved. They were eager to be led by the chief scientist.

Each man pocketed a forged passport and an airline ticket, Moscow to Rome, one way, leaving 11 p.m. tonight.

A potential buyer will be meeting them at Rome's Fiumicino Airport, the chief scientist explained. The buyer was connected to a large planetarium and was anxious to see their information. He was <u>*most*</u> *anxious to see the photographs, and make an offer there and then if satisfied.*

The three scientists were lifelong bachelors who had squirreled away every spare ruble since Friday, April 24, 1970, the day of the ill-fated Venusian probe. Money they'd entrusted to the chief scientist.

The purchases they pocketed required a substantial percentage of their life's savings. Lubricated by the Moscow Mules and giddy with hope, they toasted one another, they toasted Rome, they toasted the future, and toasted c□ачо□.

Ocean Robert Benson was already in Rome. When he had stepped off the airplane, he was elated to be in the Eternal City. Ocean was on summer break between his freshman and sophomore years in college, and had been invited to join an all-star team of under-21 soccer players in an international tournament.

But Ocean was not now happy to be in Rome. The team was faring poorly against foreign teams. Like Canadian hockey players, for whom it was said they had learned to skate before they learned to walk, these foreigners were kicking soccer balls the moment they stood up from crawling.

They called soccer football in England. *Fútbol* in Spain and Spanish-speaking nations. *Calcio* in Italy.

Many Americans didn't call soccer anything. It was outside their consciousness.

Moreover, Ocean did not start for the team, not after the first match. His performance was miserable, a performance that landed him in the coach's doghouse.

In the 87th minute, his team down 3-2, Ocean

challenged an enemy who dribbled the ball into his penalty area.

The enemy *nutmegged Ocean.

Ocean lost his cool and grabbed the enemy's jersey.

The referee blew his whistle. The enemy was awarded a penalty kick, which they converted.

At 4-2, there was no chance for an equalizer.

It was first time *ever* that Ocean began a game on the bench. When he was substituted in, a victory or even a tie was out of reach. He did not own the defensive half of the pitch as he did at home.

Ocean was not prescient, able to see half a second into the future. Too often, he was unable to see where the ball was going. His attackers, his enemy, moved the ball as if it were on a string.

He missed Quyen Wilson too. They attended the same university, her on a full academic scholarship. His soccer scholarship paid only for tuition. The full rides and the bulk of the cash in the athletic department went to the football and basketball programs.

Missing her puzzled him and disturbed him. He'd been gone a week. Why was she the focus of his homesickness? He didn't want to think beyond that.

**Nutmeg is British slang for playing the ball between an opponent's legs, for an advantage and/or to embarrass an opponent.*

≈≈≈

Quyen Wilson was not in Rome. She missed Ocean Benson as much as he missed her.

He'd been gone barely a week.

So why?

Quyen was taking biology and organic chemistry courses this summer, continuing to leap ahead of scheduled graduation. At the end of summer quarter, she'd have her BS, with a 3.85 GPA.

She'd been accepted to med school and would begin in the fall quarter.

What she wanted to be upon graduation was a general practitioner, a GP, a family doctor. Here in America, her adopted home. Or in Vietnam, where her services were in greater demand.

Much more money here, much more satisfaction there. In the United States of America, you weren't asked to treat cholera and typhoid and malnutrition and avian influenza.

Quyen Wilson was in her organic chem lab now, doing a polymer experiment, separating polypeptide macromolecules.

Her mind on Ocean, she was doing the experiment by rote.

Disturbed and puzzled.

≈≈≈

Bob Jones was not in Rome.

He was on a chaise lounge on a beach on an island in the West Indies. He was looking at the whitish band where his gold Rolex had been. Bob hoped the band would tan, matching the rest of his shriveled, liver-spotted skin.

Cheap as surgery at Caribbean medical schools (quackery mills, he thought snidely) was compared to hospitals at home, a quadruple bypass procedure was not inexpensive.

Sale of his precious Rolex had paid the last of the bills.

Little money remained. He was learning frugality the hard way.

There was not remotely enough money to repair his loose teeth. Thanks to Jim Wilson's cowardly kick in the jaw, he lived on yogurt, soft fruit, and cheese.

Jim Wilson, of whom he had nonstop homicidal thoughts. Gwen Carter Jones too.

Bob Jones was 67 years old, obviously not in the pink. He was running out of time and money to do what he yearned to do.

He needed a miracle.

As Bob absently scratched his pale wrist, the miracle came from behind him.

It plopped down on a chaise lounge beside Bob.

The miracle wore shorts and carried a cane. He was missing a foot and ankle. The plastic one replacing them had been bought on the cheap and fit badly.

On the miracle's wrist was a tattoo. The tattoo depicted twin lightning bolts, the symbol of the *Schutzstaffel*, Nazi Germany's SS. Above it, in the middle of the forearm, was a larger tattoo: Jesus crucified on a rough-cut wooden swastika.

Bob's miracle was two days late, but he had modest expectations of the man.

To make polite conversation, Bob asked him if he had a good flight.

The miracle blathered on in agonizing detail. How he missed this flight, how that connecting flight was late, how they lost his luggage.

Bob Jones did not hear a word.

≈≈≈

Jim Wilson and Gwen Carter, objects of Bob Jones' venomously obsessive hatred, were not in Rome.

They were in a time zone hours earlier than Rome's. They were home with Laura, preparing a barbecue.

Dave and Brenda Wilson and the twins were coming.

Mary Ann Benson too, bringing her non-alcoholic punch.

Richard was bringing a date, the first time the Wilsons would be meeting her. He'd had a few one-date "relationships" after his divorce five years ago. They hoped this girl was the one who finally exorcised Kelli-who-dotted-the-i-with-a-bubble.

It was a warm, sunny afternoon on this day following the summer solstice. Jim had the coals ready to start for chicken that was marinating in the refrigerator in Jim's secret sauce. Potato salad and coleslaw were prepared. Garlic bread too, wrapped in foil.

Jim had mixed feelings about these family functions. The praise and toasting of him as a hero wouldn't stop. He knew it was bolstering, out of fear of a PTSD relapse.

A year and a half ago, he'd done what he had to do, to save his mother-in-law's life.

Conquering his agoraphobia to boot.

The doorbell and telephone rang at the same time. A steady ring-ring-ring and a single ding-dong. Jim and Laura smiled. They'd never before had simultaneous callers, stereophonic visitors.

Jim went to the door to greet their first guests. He was eager to see Richard's new girl friend. Jim had more or less made peace with him. Kelli-who-dotted-the-i-with-a-bubble possessed the sexual power to corrupt guys far more worldly than his kid brother.

It wasn't Richard. It was his folks, their folks, Dave and Brenda Wilson. They were 64 and Richard was counting the days until age 65, this year on Labor Day, September 4. That was to be his last day at the body shop. They'd recently traded in their car for a pickup truck with a cab-over camper, and planned to spend the rest of the month on the road, from RV park to RV park.

Brenda brought chocolate chip cookies so freshly baked that you could smell them through the cellophane wrapping that covered the heaping dish.

As they walked through the house, Laura held the telephone out to Jim, a dazed look on her face.

It's for you.

Fearing bad news, he asked who it was and she told him.

He had to think. It was a vaguely familiar name.

Then it came to him. The director of a planetarium he'd written twice, after each of his discoveries of Venus' two moons, Aphrodite in 1965 and Gerund in 1978.

He took the phone, dazed too.

He listened, *dazed*.

N

NUBELSKI PRIZE IN SCIENTIFIC CONJECTURE.

Instituted by Rölf Nubelski (1895-1954).

Scion of a laundry bleach fortune, Nubelski devoted his life and his money to unconventional scientific experimentation.

Inspired by his attendance at the 1919 Conference on Alchemy held in the city of West Bison, Rölf Nubelski abandoned the life of a playboy and threw himself into discovering how to transmute lead into gold.

Working seven days a week in a state-of-the-art laboratory, aided by an erudite staff, Nubelski labored tirelessly for 23 fruitless years until mid-1942 when the War Department conscripted his staff and took possession of his laboratory, shifting research priority to chemical weapons.

Embittered by the seizure and the indifferent disposal of his life's work, Mr. Nubelski opened a new lab at which he explored the practicalities of a universal solvent. He soon realized that even if he did create one, he couldn't store it, as it would eat through any vessel. Otherwise, it wasn't a universal *solvent.*

He devoted the rest of his life to perpetual motion machines. This was altruism as well as a quest for scientific glory. He'd be responsible for energy production exceeding energy consumption.

Always a day away from a scientific breakthrough, he was forced into retirement by a worsening illness that was diagnosed as long-term lead poisoning.

Nubelski had spent too many years melting, boiling, combining lead into mixtures, combining it into compounds, electrolyzing, hammering, irradiating and particle-bombarding the toxic element.

Rölf Nubelski passed away at the age of 58. He never married and had no family. Before his death, he set up a trust fund that awarded an annual prize for the scientific achievement or lack thereof that most closely mirrored his own work-tilting intellectual windmills.

The award was presented each year beginning in 1960, on the anniversary of his death. It was made in West Bison, where Rölf Nubelski had had his alchemy epiphany.

In 1990, the presentation was to be on Saturday, February 10.

The 1990 winner of the Nubelski Prize in Scientific Conjecture was James Wilson.

As Jim and Laura were packing to leave for West Bison, Gwen Carter said that she remembered her mother buying Nubelski Bleach.

It came in a gallon jug with a ring handle and cost a dime.

Weird what a person remembered, she said.

Laura and Gwen had to persuade Jim to go. Had to do a hard sell on him.

He wasn't sure if it was a prize or a booby prize.

The Nubelski was given to the crackpot of the year, serious scientists and scholars claimed.

Typically, the most serious competitors for the award were creators of infomercial products.

Miraculous potions and gadgets that gave you washboard tummies and abs of iron and better-than-perfect health.

Gasoline additives that spiked economy to 75 MPG.

Software to predict stock market swings and how to get rich quick in real estate.

The winners proudly came in person to accept the Nubelski Prize in Scientific Conjecture.

The winners doing time sent proxies.

The Nobel Prize in Crackpottery, Jim Wilson thought bitterly.

Jim Wilson was ridiculed as a backyard hobbyist seeing imaginary things through a tinny, mail-order telescope that Galileo would have laughed at.

A one-eyed Vietnam vet with "issues".

Fuck them, Jim said, not for the first time.

And the horse they rode in on, Laura said, completing her husband's sentence.

The trouble started at the planetarium that phoned Jim at their 6/22/1989 backyard barbeque. A planetarium employee had met three defecting Soviet scientists who showed him compelling data and photographs by a doomed Venusian probe. They believed as Jim Wilson did, that Venus' two moons were held in suspension by a gravitational tug of war between the Sun, Venus, and the Earth.

Whether through The Politics of Scientific Envy or through genuine science, the Russians were vilified and repudiated. They had presented forged "proof" that Venus had two satellites always hidden from view.

A ruse to gain asylum and make lots of money.

The Wilsons firmly believed that the scientific community could not bear the humiliation of being proven wrong by defecting Russian scientists who drank too many Moscow Mules and by a one-eyed amateur astronomer.

It was akin to the fallout if the Nobel Prize in Literature was awarded to a mystery novelist.

This took the Russians totally by surprise. The threesome was freely spending the planetarium's money, enjoying the good life in Rome, *la dolce vita.*

Wine, women and song, easy on the tunes.

After the first news stories and the threat of a lawsuit from the planetarium that'd been hoodwinked, the chief scientist suffered a nervous breakdown.

Smack-dab on the Spanish Steps, not two meters from John Keats's house.

The police took him away as he raved about dialectical materialism and glasnost and Uncle Joe.

The other two scientists sought political asylum in Mother Russia.

The Wilsons finished packing. Jim loaded the trunk of the Impala, so Gwen could drive them to the airport for their flight, a flight that was in danger of being cancelled.

A snowstorm was predicted to clobber West Bison within twenty-four hours. The city was routinely hit by heavy snow thanks to the lake effect, where cold air from the north swept southward and picked up moisture from the large lake adjacent to the area.

All the Wilsons had to do was get there.

Jim almost voiced another objection, but if he did, he

knew that Laura would yet again remind him that a $4183.72 honorarium came with the brass-plated medal. That and free coach airfare and free cab fare to their free hotel room and free cab fare to the suburban high school auditorium for the award ceremony.

Jim had a speech prepared that nobody was going to like.

Except Laura.

It'd be their little secret.

≈≈≈

Forty-eight-year-old Oberst Skip Newt of the White Christian Minutemen had waited 18 long years for this. Reichsführer Adrian Newt, his brother, was gone. Murdered in cold blood by a deranged old man who got a slap on the wrist for this crime against humanity.

The White Christian Minutemen were kaput, leaderless, backstabbed and slandered into oblivion by an international conspiracy of Jews and Communists and faggots and darkies and slopeheads.

The man who referred to Skip Newt as a "miracle" was in Skip's opinion *Skip's* miracle. Bob Jones had searched out Skip with a private detective and located him in not the best of circumstances.

He was unemployable because of his WCM association pure and simple, Newt claimed.

Not for his police record for assault and drunkenness in public.

Not for his spotty employment history.

Not his lack of a high school diploma.

Smoke screens, they were. Discrimination against a true loyal God-fearing white American patriot.

The detective had traced Skip to his 81-year-old mother's home, where he lived in her basement and on what she was willing to share of her meager Social Security.

If Skip wasn't her youngest and sole surviving child and only living family member, he'd be out on the street.

Way back when, they'd told her she shouldn't have gone and got herself knocked up again.

They told her that her baby-making innards were plumb wore out from having five kids.

Mama spent her days upstairs watching reality TV and soap operas, wondering where she'd gone wrong raising her kids. None had made anything of themselves, but compared to Skip they were tycoons and senators.

Adrian, he was a nut case, but he had ambition. She gave him credit for that.

Skip was the old man's choice of name. The Skips of the world went to prep school or played baseball.

The old man must've been out of his skull or drunk. He was them things more than he wasn't.

Skip spent his days in the basement watching videotapes of Leni Riefenstahl's *Triumph of the Will*, her documentary of the 1934 Nuremberg Rally. Tears welling up at the power and glory of it.

He spent his evenings and nights watching Eva Braun's home movies of herself frolicking in the nude, jerking off as he did so. Party time: Him and Eva and Mary FiveFingers.

The detective pounded on his door as he was playing with himself. It was a mad scramble to get zipped up and his boner shut down without getting it caught up in his zipper.

≈≈≈

Well worth being intruded on, Skip Newt thought as he sat at a table in the cocktail lounge of the West Bison hotel where Jim Wilson and many others going to the Noodledick thing stayed, but gone now attending the prize award ceremony.

Newt was a small soft man, similar in appearance to his late Heinrich Himmleresque brother. Picked on all his life on account of his name and his looks, he was Tarzan now, he thought.

He looked out the window at the blizzard, thinking of what he'd gone and planted upstairs. Explosives were what you called your equalizer. The King of the Jungle was no match for a man with explosives.

Cane propped against a chair, Newt sat at a table, nursing a bourbon-cola, reading but not concentrating on a newspaper.

Except for the funnies, none he found funny.

Reading a paper or most else was slow going anyhow.

He nervously tapped the foot he didn't have on the floor. He still felt that gangrenous foot and ankle 18 years after its amputation. Scolded like a dimwit simple-mind by the sawbones for letting the infection go.

Same with the left nut they went and amputated the same day he got kicked in the balls by Elmer Free Carter. It itched like hell when he went too long without a bath.

Like today.

Elmer Free Carter, murdering maimer shithook, he was long gone, but his daughter and granddaughter were alive and well. The granddaughter was here with her husband, recipient of that Noodledick Prize, having it draped around his neck — Skip Newt checked his $19.95 watch — *now*.

Elmer Free Carter's granddaughter was the daughter of Bob Jones, Jones had explained. When Bob Jones set this plan into motion, Skip wondered out loud to him how he felt about his daughter very possibly dying along with the target, Jim Wilson.

Jones said he really didn't want that to happen.

Yeah, but what if it went and did happen?

Collateral damage, Jones said, shrugging. It was her fault, not *his* for staying with Pencil-neck.

Skip Newt sipped his bourbon, his hand steadier.

Bob Jones had given him the bomb materials and the know-how, lecturing him like he was a retard. It was easy, Jones said, but you had to know it so well you can do it in your sleep, so well you can get it done fast.

Unplug the small room refrigerator. Remove the light bulb. Attach one end of the wires to the socket, the other end to the grayish lump of *plastique*. The stuff looked harmless, like modeling clay. But it'd blow the fridge door and whoever opened it through the hotel wall, Jones said.

It was Skip Newt's first experience with things that went *boom*.

He'd gotten into the Wilson room with a passkey he'd snatched from a nigger maid's cleaning cart. Despite a severe case of nerves, hands shaking as he taped the wires to the light socket, he'd rigged the bomb and was in and out in under 10 minutes, breathing deeply as Bob Jones had coached, hurrying but *not* hurrying, carefully placing the plastique to the rear of all the beer and wine bottles the hotel loaded in there for you to drink so they can stick it to you on the bill.

His big brother, Reichsführer Adrian Newt, had said that The White Christian Minutemen were going to get up to speed on explosives when a fellow WCM, a safecracker and two-time loser, was released from prison.

They never had a chance to fulfill their destiny.

Newt looked at his cheap watch again. Not long, they'd be returning from their bullshit thing at the high school, on a snowmobile if they had to. Wilson had an attaboy bottle of champagne waiting in his room fridge, compliments of the hotel.

They'd taken it to his room, not five minutes after Newt finishing doing his work, a close call.

The Wilsons, up they'd go after getting back from the Nubel Bubble thing.

Up they'd go for a taste of bubbly.

Boom.

Skip Newt smiled and sipped his bourbon, nursing it.

Waiting.

≈≈≈

Jim Wilson was not accepting the Nubelski Prize in Scientific Conjecture.

He bluntly refused the medal.

His discovery was not conjecture, it was *real.*

He lectured, writing and drawing on an easel, explaining his finds and his theory that Venus' two moons were always on the planet's far side, in a gravitational tug of war between the Sun, Venus, and the Earth.

Aphrodite and Gerund. Remember those names, boys and girls.

Attendees booed and filed out.

Jim and Laura were by themselves when he finished his speech.

She hugged him, so proud of him standing up for his principles, then they filed out too.

They could shove their medal, but damned if he'd give back the $4183.72 and the rest of the perks.

Jim Wilson tended to be self-destructive at awkward times, but he wasn't crazy.

Their taxi was two blocks from the hotel now. It had four-wheel-drive and chains. West Bison folks had a handle on snow.

The Wilsons knew a bottle of free champagne awaited. They'd drink it too. They'd boogie through the lobby, up the elevator to their room.

They'd get out of their clothes and pop the cork. The hotel bed wasn't the back seat of a '62 Impala SS convertible, but it'd do.

≈≈≈

There was no *boom*, then or throughout the rest of the day and that night. The only sound emanating from the Wilsons' room was the headboard of their bed rhythmically tapping against the wall.

≈≈≈

In the morning, the snow let up. Streets were being plowed and sanded. It was as normal a day as normal was in West Bison.

Skip Newt had a leisurely breakfast, observing as the Nubelski attendees checked out, not exactly a stampede, but impatience was in the air. Jim and Laura Wilson were in the checkout line, but they could have been invisible to fellow attendees.

Skip paid his check and walked as fast as he could through snow and ice and slop to a pay phone outside a convenience store across the street, three blocks away. Not an easy task for an amputee in a rush and on a cane.

In event of a problem, Jones had ordered Newt to contact him away from the hotel, leave a message on his answering service, and wait for a call back.

Slipping and sliding and limping, Skip Newt was lucky he wasn't killed by crazy drivers. At a phone booth, after catching his breath, he pumped quarters into the slot, as many as the bitch operator told him to.

He had to stand in the icy breeze for a good 20 minutes, freezing his ass off, before the phone rang.

Bob Jones was not a happy camper, even after Skip swore he'd set the bomb correctly, following instructions to the letter.

Jones ordered him to get the goddamn fucking hell back into that room and remove the *plastique*. If he didn't and it was found in Nubelski Boy's room, the shit would hit the fan and they wouldn't be able to get close to the pencil-necked douche bag for who knows how long.

So that's what Newt sought to do. He stepped out of the elevator, and looked right and left. The foot he didn't have was aching and his arm trembling from leaning on his cane. His left nut itched like crazy.

No cleaning cart in the hallway. The stolen key card still worked. The nigger maid must've had a spare and hadn't noticed this one missing.

The room was a mess, bedding from one of the twin beds wadded up on the floor, the other made up. The champagne bottle was on the nightstand, a dead soldier. Empty beer bottles too. Disgusting, he thought as his mind flashed to nude Eva Braun, her in the bed, spread-eagled, awaiting Oberst Skip Newt. A boner developed.

Skip caught his breath, took deep breaths, hurrying but not hurrying, and as Bob Jones had endless-fucking-ly nagged him.

Skip Newt opened the fridge. He carefully reached through the forest of bottles for the *plastique*. But due to his unsteadiness, not carefully enough.

A bottle of porter fell against a loose wire. The wire that Newt hadn't taped well enough to the socket.

Almost but not quite well enough.

Dark and toasty and smoky, this brand of porter was a favorite of beer of connoisseurs, including the Wilsons, who were thirsty after the bubbly and a romp between the sheets.

Unfortunately for Skip, the Wilsons hadn't gotten around to this bottle of porter.

The porter fell against a loose wire, which Skip hadn't properly taped to the socket.

The wire touched the socket, completing the connection.

Boom.

O

OAT BRAN IS A FAD. *Don't tell Ocean Benson's Friday Night companion that! She'll bite your head off.*

Ocean and his date attended the same community college. He was majoring in general studies. A friend told him in jest that general studies meant he wasn't majoring in anything. Jocks majored in general studies and underwater basket-weaving.

Ocean didn't disagree. He was an à la carte scholar.

Ocean Robert Benson came home from Rome a changed man. He was academically and emotionally adrift, without goals.

He did know that he was done with soccer and soccer was done with him. He chose this college in part because they had no soccer team.

There were no coaches hounding him to play.

Ocean met his date, his Friday night companion, in Econ 101.

She was an English major with an emphasis on poetry.

Poetry? As far as Ocean was concerned, she had no major either. He wisely kept that to himself.

Neither was planning on taking Econ 102; he because he was an à la carte scholar, her because a section on iambic pentameter opened up.

He had not asked her out for tonight, April 26, 1991,

for her physical attractiveness. She was older and shorter and heavier than was appealing, but she had a quick wit and firm views on everything from politics to sports to their required economics textbook (it sucks!).

She said she'd go out to dinner with him if she chose the restaurant. She said it'd be a surprise and that he'd like it.

It was a surprise: a vegetarian restaurant.

Liking it? Ocean was skeptical.

The only vegetarian restaurant in this half of the state, she informed Ocean as they had before-dinner glasses of red wine.

She lectured him on the virtues of vegetarianism and how less than 2% of Americans were vegetarians. She lectured him on the importance to the diet of low-fat, high-fiber foods, and predominantly whole grains.

She lectured him on how oat bran was being tarred and feathered by know-nothings, by clueless assholes.

Ocean was two days past his 21st birthday and was feeling sophisticated, drinking wine with a worldly woman at a far-out restaurant.

She let him order for himself and applauded his choice.

She ordered the same thing — portobello cheeseburgers with fresh-cut fries.

The food came and Ocean dug in. Between halves of a toasted whole-wheat bun was a grilled portobello mushroom as big as a hamburger patty, bean sprouts, pungent white cheese, tomato, purple onion, and leaf lettuce.

The meal was so good that he lost all reservations

about vegetarian fare.

They devoured their dinners and had glasses of wine for dessert.

Ocean paid and drove her home.

She invited him into her apartment for a glass of wine.

That glass of wine became three or four or five glasses.

The new vegetarian experience led to a second new experience.

Loss of his virginity.

OMNIA MUTANTUR, NOS ET MUTAMUR IN ILLIS. *Latin for "all things are changing, and we are changing with them."*

Indeed, people and things have changed by and on Friday, May 1, 1992.

Organic farming/gardening. May Day in this climate was the recommended date to plant warm season vegetable crops, tomatoes and bell peppers and sweet corn. The soil was warm and there was no danger of a hard frost. Twenty miles out of town, 50 acres had once upon a time been homesteaded by hippies who'd been attracted by the romance of living off the land. They were long gone. After a week of backbreaking labor, organic farming was, like, man, a bad trip.

This land somehow fell into the hands of Roscoe Snails. Perhaps the endgame in a money laundering transaction to compensate him for some clandestine job he performed. Nobody knew for sure.

It was the known extent of his estate. An attorney who made a comfortable living tracing dead-end estates and contacting heirs pinpointed and telephoned Mary Ann Snails née Benson. After an absence of 14 years, she wasn't surprised to hear of Roscoe's demise, nor that he had succumbed to a still-unsolved bombing, an inactive murder investigation. The 50 acres of land was a shocker.

What to do with the land was a puzzler.

But not for long.

Ophelia, who did not dot the "i" in her name with a bubble, joined Richard Wilson in holy matrimony on a drizzly May Day on the partially-plowed and planted farm. The ceremony was to be held inside a large tent.

Ophelia was a serious young woman, pale and semi-pretty and clingy, a professional student in English literature with a special interest in Flemish poetry. Ophelia was the daughter of university English professors, who were bony and grim, with pursed lips. They were ill at ease at the rustic ceremony peopled by non-academics. The prevalent sensation was an odor of rich loam.

How primitive.

Whispered wagers were made whether Ophelia was a virgin when she began dating Richard and/or still was.

David Wilson Junior was Richard's best man. Thirty-seven years old now, he was probably a confirmed bachelor. He did date on occasion. To everybody's relief, he dated women, not men. He changed jobs twice a year. This pleased nobody, most of all himself. David Junior was also principal support and comfort today to his mother, Brenda Wilson, his arm around her as she sniffled.

Obituary notices in the local April 19, 1992 newspaper included David Wilson Senior's. At 66 years of age, David had succumbed to a heart attack while he and Brenda were traveling in their pickup truck and cab-over camper. They were finishing their first trip of the year, planning on being home in plenty of time for the wedding. Thank Heaven for small favors, as Brenda put it, that her David wasn't behind the wheel when it happened. They were at an RV park. He was putting charcoal briquettes in the barbecue at their slot when he told Brenda he felt nauseous. Then he fainted. By the time the ambulance arrived, it was too late.

On alert. That's what Jim and Laura Wilson were, at kid-brother Richard's wedding and everywhere else. They didn't consider themselves paranoid. They considered themselves vigilant and prudent. After the explosion in their West Bison hotel room, who the hell wouldn't be wary? The one fatality in the blast was identified as Skip Newt, brother of the late neo-Nazi, Adrian Newt. Laura's late grandfather had done time for killing Adrian, but the connection to the Wilsons was tenuous. Wasn't it? The police said so, but, then, what was Newt doing in their hotel room allegedly triggering a bomb that may have been intended for them? Bob Jones was an ongoing red flag, but where was he and what did he have to do with the Newts?

Gwen Carter, formerly Gwen Carter Jones, was at the wedding too. She wondered too. When the threesome held hands as the couple exchanged vows, the two women were misty-eyed, thinking of nothing but the happy couple.

Jim's single eye alternated between the happy couple and the blue sky outside and the whitish half moon visible in it. He couldn't see it, but Venus was there too, low in the horizon below the Moon, Aphrodite and Gerund in a tidy row at the planet's rear.

Ocean Benson was the last to arrive at the tent, barely making it before the couple was wed. He had dirt on his hands and under his fingernails from working the land, this morning rototilling the soil for planting, getting tomato and pepper plants and sweet corn seed in the ground. He should have been exhausted, but he wasn't. He was grateful to the girl who introduced him to manhood and vegetarianism. It was their first and last date. He'd asked her out the next week and the week after, but she brushed him off. Male conquest may've been the name of her game. Deflowering male virgins? More power to her, whatever her name was.

To Mary Ann Benson, the acreage dropped in her lap was not entirely fortuitous. Mary Ann had to pay property taxes on property she couldn't easily sell. Clinging to the last vestiges of her hippie days, she offered it to her son for payment of taxes with the provision that it would be farmed organically. She said she'd contribute $2000 at the outset for equipment and donate an old pickup truck that had been donated to BREAD, a clunker of no use that was only taking up space.

Ocean agreed, thinking he'd give it a shot for a year. Quyen was in another state for her internship and residency, and he'd dropped out of the community college, having earned few credits in any one major that applied to graduation. Ocean got to the tent, which was his tent, his living quarters, in the nick of time. His cot, camp stove, food, and organic gardening and carpentry books were stacked neatly in a corner. He was thinking how happy and honored he was that Richard and Ophelia asked him to host their marriage.

He was thinking too that judging by the warm temperature and blue sky, Ma Nature promised to give him three or four more dry days. In years past, he thought of weather strictly in terms of soccer, not for working the soil, for condition of the field, how it'd affect his planting strategy. As the minister opened his Bible, Ocean picked dirt from his fingernails, thinking that this might not be a horrible life.

One-night stand. Two days later, the lawyer for the Roscoe Snails estate was in town on other business. In a yupscale rental car, he swung by BREAD at closing time to say hi. Mary Ann sized him up: fortyish and not bad-looking. He had the start of a pot, but good hair. Nice shoulders and nice ass too. He took Mary Ann Benson to a lavish dinner that didn't spare the wine. Then to his hotel room where they screwed each other's brains out. In the morning, the severely-hungover lawyer gave Mary Ann a quick, sheepish peck on the cheek, chewed a mouthful of aspirin, and headed out for the airport. The lawyer thought he'd had a nice score, a hot one-night stand. Mary Ann was feeling just fine and not hungover. It was *her* who had the one-night stand, dinner and wine to boot. Sixty-two years old now and still a looker, she was going to have to do more of this, taking advantage of younger guys while she could.

P

PICKING THE FLYSHIT OUT OF THE PEPPER. *A classic Elmerism, thought his daughter, Gwen Carter, once she figured out what it meant.*

Priceless!

At sundown on Sunday, Independence Day, July 4, 1993, Gwen went into the hot water heater room and closed the door. She could not hear the annoying pop-bang-boom outside and she was alone with her father, Elmer Free Carter, who had been gone 17 years to the day.

In that little room with its ambiance of chlorine and nostalgia.

One of the smaller shoeboxes, an 8A, contained a single sheet of yellow-lined paper headed PICKING THE FLYSHIT OUT OF THE PEPPER.

What on earth?

Below the heading were numbered statements.

1. In the Vietnam War, they negotiated the shape of the goddamn negotiation table before they'd sit down and start talking. Meanwhile, troops on both sides were spilling buckets of blood every single goddamn day. Barrels full of it. Tanker trucks full of it.

Well, that clarified things, Gwen thought. Her father was outraged by the focus on trivia as they ignored what was important.

2. That little Dutch kid who stuck his finger in the

dike. Why the goddamn hell should he have to be out all night freezing his ass off if they'd built the thing right in the first place?

That one was harder for Gwen to decipher. Did he mean that it took a brave but trivial act to make the adults realize they had a big repair job ahead of them on their defective dike?

3. Radar. That newfangled invention we perfected around 1940 and got installed on the north end of Oahu, over there in Hawaii. On December 7, 1941, the screen filled up with dots. The operators called it in and were told no sweat, it was a flock of birds. But it wasn't birds. So why the hell have the goddamn thing there if you're not going to believe it?

The third one was a head-scratcher, but Gwen was laughing and crying so hard, she didn't care.

PSYCHIC, PUNDIT, SEER, MEDIUM, FAKIR, SWAMI, OCCULTIST, FORTUNE TELLER. *Whatever term you choose, that's how Madame Losan billed herself. Taking a trip? Marrying off a daughter? Receiving an important guest, dead or alive? Changing your hairstyle? Madame steered you through those serpentine dilemmas.*

How she did it, who can say? Numerology or astrology or the configuration of chicken entrails? Madame Losan had her secrets, her magic.

The best there is or ever was, that's what Brenda Wilson thought of Madame Losan. If you believed Brenda, Madame had ESP coming out of her ears.

Madame Losan, who claimed to connect via her crystal ball to the late David Wilson Senior.

Monday, October 31, 1994. Halloween afternoon.

Outrageous tongue-in-cheek costumes on the streets.

Witches, vampires, goblins, devils.

Jim Wilson thought that Pumpkin Day was an appropriate day for an appointment with Madame Losan. Jim and Laura persuaded Brenda to let them tag along on her appointment, to see where Madame Losan was coming from, why she was so expensive, costing his mom money she didn't have to spare.

Dave Senior hadn't been able to put much aside from his wages as a body and fender man. Even though they traveled modestly in their camper truck, Jim's parents spent all their Social Security and what his tiny union pension brought in.

Madame Losan's studio was in an old part of the city. It wasn't *too* grimy, seedy, or dangerous at night, and had its share of trendy restaurants.

The ambience was on the button for a fortune teller seeking an upmarket clientele.

Madame practiced the occult on the second floor above a *pho* shop. Her door was open for her client.

She sat in a wicker chair at an ornate wooden table behind a curtain of beads.

Madame was leathery and of indeterminate age. She dressed in layers of black silk, a red bandanna, and clanging silver bracelets.

Madame Losan wore a trick-or-treat outfit every day, Jim Wilson thought, flashing back to Vietnam, where every day had been Halloween for PFC James Wilson, a Halloween where every home gave the trick-or-treaters popcorn balls containing razor blades.

Madame caressed the crystal ball on her table and said that she *knew* that Brenda wasn't coming alone.

Isn't that amazing, said Jim, who asked Madame if she were Vietnamese.

Hardened by the sarcasm, Madame asked why he asked.

No particular reason. Are you?

Madame was obviously insulted. She said that she was from that region, but from nowhere they could know unless they were geographically astute. Her homeland was known as the Fourth Indochina, after Laos, Cambodia and Vietnam. It was landlocked, surrounded by China, Burma, Thailand and Laos, the only Indochinese nation the Communists didn't take over. She wasn't a boat person, but left anyhow for a better life here with normal persons and the mentally unbalanced.

With every word, she was staring at Jim. Mocking him.

A slam at Jim and his Venusian moons and his PTSD?

Her homeland as imaginary as his Aphrodite and Gerund?

How much had Mom told this hag?

He and Laura weren't poor, but they were in what might be deemed professional ruts. Her stuck in a midlevel software job, under a glass ceiling, ancient at 51. Nerdish little boys shooting up past her, age discrimination a growing probability every single day.

Him at BREAD, happy in his niche, unhappy that he was going nowhere faster than fast at the state's minimum wage of $4.25 per hour.

He didn't ask for a raise, though Gwen and Mary Ann would grant him one.

If he took more, there'd be less to give.

Had Madame Losan done a credit report on them? Concluding that they were financially conservative and not affluent, unlikely to squander their discretionary income on her juju.

Therefore, there was nothing in it for her to be diplomatic, Jim thought.

She had her tentacles firmly attached to his mom, one sucker in the family.

Madame moved along, hand on her globe, eyes half closed, reptilian-like. She was hearing Brenda's David, unseen in woods adjacent to an RV park. Talking to his beloved Brenda, telling how much he missed her and not to worry, he was in a good place. He was with many seniors, who were good and supportive company.

This is what had amazed Jim's mom, how Madame had heard him there, when no one else could.

Arms folded, Jim shook his head in disgust, not trying to hide his contempt. For Chrissake, everyone knew his dad died at an RV park and that many have at least a slender greenbelt bordering them. The great out-of-doors for those who drive here and there to be semi-close to nature.

Trick or treat.

Madame stopped talking and abruptly let loose of the crystal ball, as if it were electrified.

How dare you, you rude and stupid and reckless man! You come into my studio and insult me. See what you have done? You have agitated Mr. Wilson. He has run off, deep deep into the forest. He might never return!

Jim said that he hadn't said a word, that she must be reading his mind.

Brenda Wilson turned to her son, presenting the disapproving frown she did when he misbehaved as a child.

He held his mother's hand and kissed her cheek.

Apologize to me, Madame ordered.

Jim smiled at Madame.

Madame said, very well, you asked for it. I am putting a curse on you.

Jim Wilson laughed out loud, slapping his knees.

Laura Wilson covered her mouth with both hands so she didn't laugh out loud or call Old Lady Losan a string of four-letter names.

You will not laugh when pustulating lumps appear. Do not waste money on treatment. It will be hopeless.

Brenda ever protective of her son, turned to Madame Losan, and asked her to please remove the curse. He was a naughty boy, but he doesn't deserve this. Not sores and lumps.

Never. Even if he begs me on his hands and knees.

Well, Brenda Wilson said, you have shown your true colors. You're a bully and a liar. My Dave wouldn't give a nasty, mean person like you the time of day!

Then she and her checkbook walked out in a huff.

Jim told Madame Losan to have a nice day and followed.

Jim and Laura spent time with Brenda in the next few days, finally convincing her for good that Madame was a 100-percent, 24-karat gold-plated fraud, a swindler who preyed on the vulnerable.

Unbeknownst to anybody, first thing in the morning on those next days, Jim Wilson locked himself in the bathroom, got naked, and checked himself for pustulating sores.

Using a hand mirror to examine every square inch of skin.

Q

QUADRICENTENNIAL, A: THURSDAY FEBRUARY 29, 1596 – THURSDAY FEBRUARY 29, 1996. *Nothing much happened on either day or on any other February 29. Which was understandable, as February 29 was a leap day, occurring once every four years. If you wanted to be technical, 2/29/1596 – 2/29/1996 was a CENTENNIAL.*

The nuts and bolts of it was this. The Earth whizzed around the Sun once every 365.24219 days (compared to 224.7 days for Venus and its two moons), so if every year was 365 days, eventually July would be in the dead of the northern hemisphere winter.

That's why you have to tack on an extra day every four years.

And that's not all. In the Gregorian calendar that most of us use? It wasn't astronomically correct to add a leap day every *four years. Tweaking was required, namely having a February 29 only in years evenly divisible by 400, i.e.: the year 2000 yea, the year 1900 nay.*

Actually, two things happened on February 29, 1996. A birth and a near-death, each with a touch of the mysterious and the illicit and a surprise.

Ophelia Wilson gave birth to a seven pound, nine ounce son named Richard Wilson Junior. As she held the newborn, the proud father sat in the delivery room with her, beaming.

Or was he sitting out in the waiting room, biting his nails?

Ophelia had an ultra-secret hang-up about twins. No, not like Dr. Mengele and his ghastly experiments on them at Auschwitz, nothing like that at all.

Ophelia, her and her Victorian persona, *craved* sex.

To put it crudely, she was hornier than a three-peckered goat.

She was hornier than a prison ward of sex offenders.

She was hornier than if she mainlined Spanish fly.

No one man could satisfy her.

However, Ophelia believed strongly in the sanctity of marriage and desired to be a wife. The only conceivable solution to her problem, her sexual/matrimonial conflict, was to marry an identical twin.

Her rationale: If she was sleeping with each, wasn't she sleeping with just one? Who could say with certainty that twins weren't God's doppelgängers? Accordingly, she was cheating on her husband without cheating on her husband.

Richard continued beaming as Ophelia held the baby boy. Whether the boy's father was beside her or in the waiting room, was that really really relevant at this blessed moment?

≈≈≈

The second thing that happened on February 29, 1996 took place on a tropical island in the West Indies. It was paradise to some, hell to others.

The latter to Bob Jones.

Age 74, looking older and feeling older, Jones decided to end it all.

Many of his teeth had fallen out, courtesy of Pencil-neck Wilson's cowardly kick in the jaw. He had angina pectoris and was in frequent pain. His medicines were running low and he could get no more. Bob Jones owed everybody on the island, and no further credit was to be extended.

Jones lived in a small shack in a part of the island's town that no tourist dared visit. His neighbors preyed on one another and those who blundered in. They vandalized and looted Bob's shack until there was little left to damage or rip off.

His most valuable piece of personal property was a small refrigerator. Bob theorized that the vultures let it be, preferring to steal its contents.

Permitting the hen to live to continue laying eggs to steal.

On this February 29, Bob unplugged the fridge, placed his last lump of *plastique* inside it, removed the light bulb, ran wires from the *plastique* to the socket, closed the door, and plugged it back in.

He grasped the handle, thinking that this was a fitting and ironic way to go.

Then Bob had an inspiration.

He had several cans of beer in the fridge. He unplugged, removed one, and plugged back in. He drank it, leaving the empty on his small table for any passerby to see.

Cheese in a mousetrap.

Exhausted by the activity, he crawled into bed, a cot in

an alcove behind a raggedy curtain. The savages did not fear him, committing their crimes if he was home or not. In the daytime or at night.

They did not disappoint. Shortly before sunset, a pair of scrawny colored boys came in, and went right to the fridge.

Bob Jones smiled. He'd check out his way, taking the thieving dinges with him.

He closed his eyes and listened to the refrigerator open.

He listened to the clanking of cans.

He listened to the refrigerator door slam shut. He listened to laughter and island patois as they left with their booty.

What the hell happened?

What the fucking hell *didn't* happen?

Bob got up and went to the fridge and opened the door. The light didn't come on.

He tried the room light. It didn't come on.

Now Bob Jones knew.

Talk about timing.

His electricity had been cut off for nonpayment.

His death was a non-death, he thought bitterly.

Life wasn't fair even when he was trying to end it.

QUICHE LORRAINE. *Ocean Benson's quiche lorraine wasn't your mother's quiche lorraine. His was a hearty meal, yes, but it didn't have a trillion calories and a billion grams of fat and 5000 times your daily recommended allowance of cholesterol.*

On September 28, the last nice Sunday of 1997, Ocean invited Quyen Wilson out to his organic farm for dinner. Next to a small fridge, on a small stove and oven inside the tent, powered by a small generator, he made:

OCEAN'S QUICHE LORRAINE

1 whole-wheat pie crust. You may have to go to a health food store to find one. Think of white flour or any other milled grain as poison. Toxic.

1 finely chopped onion.

3 beaten eggs or 1 ½ cups egg substitute.

1 ½ cups of shredded low-fat Swiss or cheddar (your preference).

No bacon.

1 cup 2% milk. No half-and-half or heavy cream.

1 tbsp. Dijon mustard.

¼ tsp. salt. No more. Salting your food should be the diner's option. You can make food saltier but it's tough to make it unsaltier.

1 tsp.freshly-ground black pepper.

Pour mixture evenly into the pie crust that's in a pie tin, glass or metal.

Bake in preheated oven at 375° for 30-40 minutes or until a dinner knife stuck in the center comes out clean.

Enjoy.

If it's not quite to your liking, experiment with ingredients and cooking time and with herbs and spices.

Anything you like in your spice cabinet will work in quiche lorraine. Fresh herbs from your garden are the best.

They ate Ocean's quiche lorraine inside the tent, seated on folding chairs at his workbench. He'd lit a candle in the center. The meal was accompanied by a white zin Quyen brought that had been recommended by her mother.

A well Ocean had dug provided fresh water. Beside the tent and a chemical toilet was the framework of a cabin. Ocean was hurrying to get the walls and roof done before winter. He'd finish the interior then.

He spoke of other plans, some of which Quyen thought might be grandiose.

But Ocean had surprised her before.

He spoke of having gravitated completely to vegetarianism. It wasn't as if he was making some kind of save-the-planet statement. It was a personal choice. Animal protein had been less and less appealing. When the sight of raw red meat in a butcher's counter made him queasy, he knew it was time.

Doing it because he wanted to, gravitating to it, not knowing exactly why. He wasn't defensive, justifying it, selling it. Vegetarianism wasn't a leftover hippie affectation, back-to-the-land bullshit.

It was his lifestyle.

It was him.

In season, he had fresh vegetables on the table every day. He was putting up his garden surplus in mason jars for the off-season.

Dr. Quyen Wilson applauded him. She didn't eat meat every day, but when she wanted a steak, she *wanted* a steak.

Dr. Wilson was finishing her residency, working in the emergency ward of a large hospital. She had seen too many people bought in because of clogged arteries.

Alive.

Barely alive.

Or DOA.

Too morbid, she said. Let's change the subject.

They tried but neither felt like talking. They finished the wine and Ocean opened a bottle of merlot he had in his fridge. Quyen joked that red wine had to be served at room temperature. Ocean joked that he didn't have a room.

A breeze wafted through, blowing out the candle.

It's trying to tell us something, Quyen said.

Yes it is, Ocean said, as he zipped up the tent flaps.

R

RADIOLOGIST RENUMERATION, RANGE OF. *The income of a radiologist had a wide range, depending on experience, location and variety of skills. In 1998, the median was roughly $250,000.*

Thirty-year-old Dr. Quyen Wilson had it all. If you asked around in the local medical community, she was a living legend. They said Dr. Wilson had X-ray vision, able to see on X-rays and MRIs and ultrasounds and any other subspecialty beyond what she could *see.*

In med school, her rare talent was first recognized in an elective radiology course.

Henceforth, she had been steered and high-pressured into that specialty, all but physically pushed and shoved and booted.

For the greater good of humanity.

Quyen believed it was a crock that had snowballed, her an urban legend of sorts. Yes, she scored in the 99th percentile in testing and performance, but that did not give her X-ray vision like Superman (who she fondly remembered in her eight-year-old Superman/gunpowder fantasy).

Up, up and away!

Suspicious that those in top administration had a hidden agenda — a gender quota to fill or whichever — she buckled.

So a radiologist she was.

Dr. Wilson worked six long days a week. She had little time to regret being sidetracked from her original goal to be a GP in Vietnam. Or her present goal of being a GP at home.

Vietnam was halfway around the world, an alien place she'd struggle to communicate in a language she didn't know. A socialist country with tight restrictions on citizens and visitors alike.

No question, there was a crying need for her at home too.

She took Sundays off, looking forward to them especially in the summer. Helping Ocean Benson on his 50-acre organic farm was a relaxing and exhausting joy.

Six years after Ocean's mother sold him the farm for taxes, a $2000 grubstake, and a beater of a pickup truck, you'd never know it from the photos she had seen of Ophelia's and Richard's wedding.

The tent was now covered storage space and the cabin was done.

A larger generator provided electricity.

The chemical toilet was gone. An enclosed bathroom in a corner of the cabin had a hot water tank, a toilet, and a bathtub with a handheld shower.

On the downside, a county tax assessor, a conscientious (read: chickenshit) civil servant, had driven by and seen that Shaggy Neglected Rustic was Efficient Suburban Agriculture. The hike in property taxes was a fist to the gut. But nothing Ocean couldn't handle. In a way.

How did Ocean afford this? He didn't. Like the majority of farmers everywhere, large and small, he was in hock.

His mother, Mary Ann, dropped by now and then, giving encouragement and pulling weeds till her back throbbed. There was a widowed gentleman across the road, a retired aeronautical engineer. She struck up a friendship with him.

On his mother's visits, Ocean saw her car parked across the road in the following morning.

His *68-year-old* mother.

Ocean couldn't help but smile.

Ocean Robert Benson was living proof that one could be happy with a new dream. He had gone forward from soccer.

He had built a small hen house. Chickens ran around (free range, he joked), eggs for Ocean, protein supplementing the blocks of cheese he bought on sale when he ran into town weekly in that scabrous old pickup. When the hens were too old to lay, he butchered them and gave them to his mom for BREAD donations.

Could Dr. Quyen Wilson, *not* a general practitioner, do the same? Not the same, but the same. Meaning doing what she wanted to do with her life.

Good question.

On this Sunday, June 13, 1998, cool season crops like peas were at their peak, in abundance. The first of the warm season vegetables too — cherry tomatoes and young asparagus. Thanks to word of mouth, Ocean Farm (never mind the oxymoron) was hugely popular.

On sales day, Sunday afternoons, 1 p.m. to 5 p.m. cars were parked on the narrow highway's shoulders, as many as 20 at a time.

Dragging themselves to the cabin with the little produce they didn't sell, Quyen wondered what Ocean had cleared. He probably didn't know either. He made change out of his blue jeans and shirt pockets and stuffed the bills in them.

Dr. Wilson guessed $300. That before seed and fertilizer (Wait, no, he'd chew your head off. He was organic all the way, with mulch and companion planting) and gas for the tiller. He cleared $150, if that.

She earned above the average for a radiologist, doing so well that her student loans were paid off. She earned in an hour what Ocean did in a week. A growing-season week. How did he survive in January?

She envied him.

She couldn't wait for Sunday to roll around.

Ocean had installed low-tech solar heating on the roof of his cabin, black plastic stapled to wooden frames, plastic tubing inside. On this warm sunny day, a week and a day from the solstice, the collectors produced enough hot water to fill Ocean's bathtub.

What Ocean and Quyen did before and after they bathed together was not incest, Dr. Wilson explained. Not biologically. Different genes and chromosomes. They weren't even first or second or third cousins, biologically or otherwise.

That they were raised as honorary cousins or siblings was moot. In any event, too many passionate Sundays had gone by to undo it, to chalk it up to a single mistake, an indiscretion.

They ended the pointless discussion and the irrational guilt, by soaping each other's back.

S

SUNDAY MAY BE A DAY OF REST, BUT THIS SUNDAY AND THE SATURDAY BEFORE, JANUARY 1, 2000, WERE DAYS OF RELIEF. DAYS THAT LED TO FINGER-POINTING, SOME FAIRLY, SOME UNFAIRLY.

We knew that Y2K was shorthand for the year 2000 A.D. We didn't know if 3000 A.D. will be Y3K.

Nor care.

Thanks to the Y2K hysteria, Laura Wilson had smashed through the glass ceiling, age discrimination overruled by her number-crunching prowess, intelligence and proficiency.

But Laura's finger-pointing got the better of her.

The best job of her life came to a sudden end on the past November 24, the day before Thanksgiving, when she was booted from her senior software manager position.

Many people believed that electronic doomsday was a month and a week away. In the computer olden days and Middle Ages, in the 1960s and 1970s and 1980s, when memory was slight and expensive, programmers economized by using two digits for a year rather than four. The widespread fear was that when 2000 rolled around, computers would interpret it as 1900, a humongous glitch that will cause all major industries to go kablooey.

Worldwide, estimates of money spent to correct the problem ran as high as $300 billion. Lately, Laura's former employer earned the bulk of its income doing Y2K repair jobs.

Lucrative Y2K repair jobs.

Numbers and computer code were no match for Laura Wilson. She managed three repair teams and stepped in to put out fires.

Laura soon came to believe that half of the fixes were unnecessary. She felt guilty as hell. Guilty and increasingly angry.

Goddamn fucking pissed!

Laura Wilson outlined in detail the esoteric reasons why half their clients were flushing their money down the crapper.

Her reasons caused spots to appear before a lay person's eyes.

But sharp techies got it in short order.

She had trouble controlling her anger and concomitantly, keeping her mouth shut, spouting off to friends and coworkers that her company behaved like pigs at a trough.

The word slipped out to clients. If they heard after the work was done, *they* were pissed. Brutally pissed.

If they heard beforehand, they cancelled the work.

By and by, the word slipped out to Laura's upper management. They confronted her.

Not only didn't Laura deny the accusations to save her job, she asked them why *they* weren't feeling guilty.

Laura Wilson was given 15 minutes to clean out her

office. In case she forgot the way to the parking lot, Security escorted her.

Y2K came.

The technological world did not come to an end.

Not a whole helluva lot happened, proving that the threat was somewhat exaggerated. That Y2K was on a Saturday instead of a weekday didn't hurt either. Laura was vindicated, but her income was zip, not in the six-figures it was a month and a week earlier.

However, she'd walked out of there with company stock options worth $5.7 million. A nest egg the size of a pterodactyl egg.

Y2K or no Y2K, January 1 was New Year's Day, a national holiday and date of many college bowl games. For their viewing pleasure, Jim Wilson hung a television from the ceiling of their garage. Also, over time, Jim had insulated the garage and fashioned a heating duct from their natural gas furnace. It had become a rec room/garage.

Toasty and comfortable and bare-ass-naked, the Wilsons drank champagne and watched football in the back seat of their 1962 Chevrolet Impala convertible. When they weren't doing other stuff.

Living on their savings and his meager wage at BREAD, they toasted each other.

Today, without a care in the world.

But an uncertain tomorrow.

They debated for the umpteenth time whether or not to roll the $5.7 million into a safe instrument like government bonds. Piddling interest rate, but safe.

The NASDAQ continued soaring to the moon, so why

should they?

On the other hand—

Jim reached over the seat into the glove box for change they kept for bridge and highway tolls. He brought out a 1999 quarter. It featured the State of Connecticut on the reverse side.

How about it, he said, heads we sell, tails we keep?

Flip it, big boy.

He stuck the arm attached to the hand that had five fingers outside the back seat and flipped the quarter.

≈≈≈

On Y2K, Bob Jones was sick and destitute in his tropical paradise. He slept on the beach and in alleyways. In the town, he begged for pocket change from tourists.

One woman handed him a lottery ticket she'd found in her husband's pants before giving them to the hotel laundry.

Bob Jones cursed her, calling her a twat, telling her it was a sick fucking joke.

She paled and walked off, wasting no time.

But Bob hung on to the ticket.

Eighteen hours later, as he was curled up on the beach, Bob Jones's system gave out. At age 78, unloved, neither missed nor would he be mourned, the Flea Killer Edison lived longer than he deserved to.

A beachcomber came upon his body at dawn and went through his pockets.

He brought home a few coins and the lottery ticket.

His wife practiced voodoo. She studied the ticket as they smoked ganja. She told him what she saw sandwiched inside the ticket.

A wafer of pure gold.

The beachcomber didn't know how a piece of cardboard could have an interior wafer of gold, but he replied with a shrug. He was used to her talking that way to her customers. With her hexes and her charms, she made much more money than he did, so he accepted *wafer of pure gold* as the truth.

She told him to mail the ticket to the address of the United States lottery office on the back of it.

He did.

A week later, they received a special delivery letter from the lottery office asking if they wanted their $5.7 million in a lump sum after taxes or in 25 annual installments.

Robert Jones was buried in a pauper's grave. The grave had no headstone other than a large rock to indicate that the space was taken.

His death was announced in the local newspaper: Bob Jones, USA, age 75-80?

≈≈≈

Bob Jones's West Indies island *was* paradise to an American tourist couple. At a beachfront palapa bar, a server brought their drinks, sweet concoctions that came with an umbrella and chunks of fruit on a stick.

The server asked where they were from.

The man laughed and said The Great White North.

The server forced a smile, having heard that one no more than 10,000 times.

The woman picked up a newspaper that had been left on the bar. She showed her husband Bob Jones's tiny obit and said that Laura Wilson had spoken of her father at lunch one day when they were on the subject of parents.

The woman worked for Laura on one of her Y2K repair crews. She thought Laura's firing was unfair, but she kept her feelings to herself. The woman had too good a job to lose.

Laura had snidely referred to hers as Father Sir, a hateful man. A fugitive from the law for years, his name was Bob Jones.

Although there was no shortage of Bob Joneses in the world, the man said she should call Laura Wilson when they got home.

The woman said she'd do it.

The couple had a wonderful two weeks on the island and completely forgot about the died-in-paradise Bob Jones.

≈≈≈

David Wilson Junior found his calling.

He lived in a district near downtown that was undergoing spasms of gentrification. Transients and financial planners coexisted. Union halls and boutiques too. High-end jewelry stores sharing a common wall with taverns where anything could happen. A tattoo parlor next to a restaurant with a cutesy name in neon and candles on the tables for the expense account lunch crowd.

David lived and worked at the 20th and top floor of a new condo. He'd paid a bundle for the pad. It looked out at the city skyline and if he lowered his eyes, at the old brick building across the street.

It and its dumpy apartments for pensioners and assorted losers.

The slum ought to be bulldozed, he thought. It hurt his

property value.

David Wilson Junior worked at home, prospering as a day trader, making thousands of dollars per day picking winners, and most listings were.

It was like hitting the winner on every horse race.

Like a slot machine that paid off on every spin.

A cornucopia, it was.

A horn of plenty.

Today was Y2K and the stock markets were closed.

Any day the markets were closed were days of mourning to David Wilson Junior.

David dealt by sipping $80 brandy and watching sports on the most expensive, biggest-screen TV sold.

The only time his mind wasn't on Ophelia and the baby, was when he thought of the money he'd accumulated on paper: $5.7 million.

Or should the kid be David Wilson III?

Ophelia was coming up later on, having made some excuse to his brother/her husband, who'd be babysitting the three-year-old.

That he was sexually addicted to her was the mother of all understatements.

Five-point-seven mil.

Fat city, baby!

Might be a good time to cash some in. Maybe set up a trust fund for the kid in some dull, rock-solid low yield. A secret trust fund he'd surprise his son/nephew with when it was time to start college.

On the other hand.

Who knows what inflation would do to $5.7 million and a low interest rate over the years. The smart thing was to keep building his pile of cash, to keep mining that rich vein of pure gold.

His buzzer buzzed.

David Junior jumped out of his chair and buzzed Ophelia in.

SYZYGY, A #@%&. *The straight-line alignment of three heavenly bodies. In our solar system, the sun, moon and earth was an example.*

The #@%& adjective was Jim Wilson's compromise to Laura, who preferred the real obscenities. She bought his argument that her choice words will send his letters flying into the wastebasket even faster. It was Monday, October 25, 2001, the 36th anniversary of his discovery of Aphrodite, the larger of Venus's two moons.

Jim Wilson, age 55 and not getting any younger, was composing a letter to the planetariums, newspapers and major universities, reminding them of his discovery.

He did not write the newsreel companies.

There were none to write.

He wrote to what had replaced them – TV news networks and cable TV channels and talk radio.

Laura was behind him, hands on his shoulders, kissing his neck when he finished.

Just because the #@%&s were stupid was no reason to forget that you weren't stupid.

T

TWENTY MONTHS AND THREE WEEKS HERETOFORE, THE 1999 QUARTER ROLLED UNDER THE 1962 CHEVROLET IMPALA TO THE RIGHT FRONT TIRE WHERE IT CAME TO REST LEANING AGAINST IT.

Jim Wilson got on his belly and shined his flashlight at President Washington's profile. The State of Connecticut was touching rubber.

What were the odds of that?

Laura and Jim Wilson obeyed the whim of the quarter and did this:

On Monday, January 3, 2000, 20 months ago, they invested half the $5.7 million of Laura's stock options in United States Savings Bonds.

This was entirely Jim's idea. His late dad and his 76-year-old mom had given him and his brothers a $25 Savings Bond on their birthdays until they turned 18. The interest was negligible in his childhood as it was in the early Twenty-first Century.

Jim's reasoning was threefold:

1. The bonds were safer than safe. If the bonds defaulted, the United States Treasury crashed and burned too. That was unlikely and, if so, was as devastating as an asteroid closing in on the earth.

2. Think of the 27 men in the mess tent. It was

patriotic too. No PTSD, he assured the love of his life. It's what was in his heart.

3. He hadn't the foggiest notion how and why he'd thought of this. A wild hunch.

And did she have a better idea?

Laura didn't have a better idea. They purchased $10,000-denomination United States Savings Bonds, an inches-thick stack. They went straight into a bank safe deposit box.

By today, Monday, September 10, 2001, the other $2.85 million would've been doomed, bursting with the tech bubble if they'd ridden along with Laura's former employer, a monetary kamikaze.

The Wilsons had shuffled it around, spending, paying taxes on it and the other half, spending, adding a half bath to their old rambler, spending, paying Jim's mother's house off and buying her a new car too, spending, upgrading to a top-of-the-line hobbyist telescope, spending, donating to BREAD, spending.

The good: Age discrimination was somebody else's problem.

The not-so-good-but-not-terrible: What to do with the rest of their lives?

The bad: N/A.

They went around the world, a 30-day package that cost two-thirds of Laura's last annual salary, seeing places they'd always wanted to see and places they'd never heard of.

Panama and the Canal, Grenada, Rio, Barcelona, Tangier, London, Paris, Copenhagen, Budapest, Mumbai, Angkor Wat, Ho Chi Minh City, Sydney, Easter Island, the

Galápagos Islands, Machu Picchu, Copán, Tikal.

≈≈≈

David Wilson lost his boodle when the tech bubble burst.

Picture the Vegas degenerate gambler, the schmuck the casinos pray on their knees for.

He's the one who keeps a notebook of numbers the roulette wheel lands on, *knowing* there is a pattern.

He's the one who *knows* that the way to turn his luck around is to double up in the next game.

He's the one who's going to clean out the house at the blackjack table by card counting, the one who moves his lips as he does, and is shown the sidewalk after half a deck.

He's the one who doesn't notice that Vegas pawn shops take in *everything*, from wedding rings to RVs.

David Wilson, day trader, chased his money as the NASDAQ tumbled off a cliff. Chased the foulest, rankest, fastest-falling issues, buying shares at bargain prices, to capitalize when they came out of their vertical dives.

By September 10, 2001, David had lost it all.

The condo, the big-screen TV, and Ophelia Wilson.

David was drinking $8 brandy now (exactly 10% of $80 sauce; the ratio taunted him), drinking way too much of it.

Ophelia Wilson had been out of his life for months, him a drunk who had frightened her and/or was unable to get it up.

On September 10, 2001, David Wilson was living across the street in the old brick building, with the pensioners and assorted losers.

His view from his daylight-basement window was

partially obscured by the planter box, even though urine had shriveled the vegetation. He could barely see his former digs. On a foggy day, nothing above the 15th floor was visible.

He didn't know how anything could get worse for anybody.

≈≈≈

Gwen Wilson and Mary Ann Benson spent their September 10, 2001 at BREAD, taking turns on the forklift and out front. Demand was up, donations down. Dot-commers were lined up with the indigent.

As Mary Ann was bringing down a pallet of canned soup, Ocean Benson and Dr. Quyen Wilson were closing the rear doors of Ocean's van. During the summers, she worked three days a week as a radiologist and three days a week at Ocean Farm.

On Sundays, they locked a chain across the foot of the driveway.

Sundays were theirs and theirs alone.

On that September 10th, the van was filled with sweet corn, green beans, and ripe tomatoes the size of baseballs. They were taking the produce to BREAD.

Ocean got behind the late-model van that was in his name, but paid for by Quyen. As were the vegetables in it.

He drove down the rutted driveway and onto the highway. He didn't feel like a kept man. Her money went to a good cause, not to him.

TTTYIBUALIRCDNISE OF TTMARE. *Or unjumbled, INDESTRUCTABILITY OF MATTER*

An example of matter's indestructibility. Toss a log into a fireplace on a stormy February evening as Jim Wilson did on Saturday, February 16, 2002.

Then get back on the sofa beside Laura, woolen blanket covering them.

Drinking hot cocoa, mesmerized by the red-hot, crackling fire.

The log was dry.

It quickly burned to ashes.

Up the chimney it went.

Sparks, smoke, gases, vapors.

Gone but not gone; molecules were scrambled into different forms.

Same as an off-course Venusian probe that plunged into the hottest fireplace of all, the sun. El Sol.

That and a comet speeding to a fiery death.

The comet that contributed to a discovery of Aphrodite.

U

U-2003 WASHED UP AGAINST THE ROCKS ON THE ISLAND OF SUDOESTE ISLA DURING A WINTER STORM ON THE NIGHT OF JULY 8, 2003.

Sudoeste Isla Island was in the southwest Atlantic, 200 miles off the Uruguayan coast. It was rocky and crescent-shaped, with a land area of 14 square miles. Nothing was native to it but moss and a few species of sea bird.

Sudoeste Isla Island was inhabited by six men operating a small weather station. The storm of Tuesday July 8 was the most violent winter occurrence recorded since the weather station was built in 1964.

Winds reached 95 miles per hour. Waves washed over half the island.

The storm dislodged U-2003 with such force that it ended up 50 feet inland, on its side.

A metallic beached whale.

When the submarine was discovered the next day, the weather station personnel assumed that it had sunk late in World War II in similar storm conditions and wedged against rocks below the surface.

With the aid of pry bars and a sledgehammer, the weather personnel were able to open the hatch. Skeletal remains of 15 people were removed. Twelve of them wore tattered *Kriegsmarine* (Nazi Navy) uniforms, four officers and eight men.

The other three were civilians, two men and one woman. They wore civilian clothes and carried Paraguayan passports issued in Spanish names.

Despite some cosmetic changes, the photographs on the passports were unmistakable.

Adolf Hitler

Eva Braun.

Martin Bormann.

≈≈≈

On the night of Tuesday July 8, 2003, Jim Wilson aimed his upgraded telescope at Venus. It was a warm, starry night. Venus was clearer than ever, much larger and brighter than it had been with the old telescope.

Venus was all he saw.

≈≈≈

While Jim stood on the patio, patiently waiting for Aphrodite and Gerund, Laura Wilson surfed the Internet, screening charities. Jim was in full agreement that giving worthy charities a $10,000 United States Savings Bond was a terrific idea. It was just a matter of finding the right ones.

≈≈≈

A Chinese probe that'd been launched to study the outer planets attempted to circle the sun to increase velocity by what is known as the "gravitational slingshot effect". On July 8, 2003, China's mission control lost contact with the probe on the far side of Venus and never regained it.

They determined correctly that they miscalculated the

probe's trajectory, allowing it to be diverted by Venus's gravitational tug.

They determined incorrectly that the probe slammed into Venus.

≈≈≈

Brenda Wilson, age 78, gave comfort and support to her 48-year-old son David, rather than vice versa. He'd moved in to his remodeled childhood home, living on the largesse of her Social Security and help from brother Jim.

David hated every minute of it, hating how Jim looked down on him. He hated himself too.

They had been in the living room watching TV, the national news. David hated all television except reality TV, so he went into his childhood (and present bedroom) to sneak a swig of brandy.

He heard Mom cry out. He thought she may have fallen, trying to get out of her rocking chair.

He hurried into the living room and listened to her goofy tale of a special news bulletin. The bodies of Adolf Hitler, Eva Braun, and Martin Bormann had been found in a submarine that washed onto a faraway island by South America.

David listened politely, looking at the TV, which was in a commercial for Nubelski Bleach. It came in a plastic jug, without a ring handle.

If his mother was coming down with Alzheimer's, what the hell was he going to do?

If they had to take Mom away to a nuthouse, would Jim let him stay here?

≈≈≈

Mary Ann Benson, age 73, did not watch the news, did

not know that the Nazi remains had been found. The widowed gentleman across the road from Ocean's organic farm, the retired aeronautical engineer, may or may not have watched the news. He was on a cruise arranged by the local senior activities center.

Mary Ann hadn't seen him for a few weeks, so she dropped by to say hello and learned he was on the cruise.

His 19-year-old grandson was keeping an eye on the house.

Mary Ann and the grandson chatted. The grandson went to the fridge for bottles of Grandpa's beer, getting one for himself and one for her.

The old broad had a nice bod for her age, the boy observed. With each successive longneck, her skin tightened and her gray hair darkened. Her tits rounded and gained altitude.

The youngster had nice arms and a flat gut and was kind of cute, Mary Ann observed. With each successive longneck, he matured physically. His abs flattened and his biceps grew.

He matured emotionally too, in spite of his conversation centering on gross-out frat house parties. Projectile vomiting contests. Mooning the sorority house across the street. And the like.

One thing led to another, her showing him the way.

When they finished, him much too quickly, he told Mary Ann that he loved her.

Oh shit, Mary Ann Benson thought. Not only have I robbed the cradle, I popped his cherry.

Him a minor.

Possibly a crime in 25 states.

Mary Ann vowed to cease this behavior. She wanted to make excuses, get her sluttish ass out of there and across the road. She wanted to let him down gently, pleading a headache or heart pain, something befitting her age. Telling this sweet child she loved him too.

Before she could, the kid's batteries recharged and he was all over her.

It'd be impolite not to stick it out for the night, so she did.

She'd be a story for the boy to pass around the frat house, a granny so hot she oughta be in the *Guinness Book*.

Mary Ann could live with that.

V

VEGETARIANISM HAS VARIATIONS. DECEMBER 7, 2005.

A pescetarian will eat seafood. A vegan will not eat any animal or dairy product. A flexitarian occasionally eats meat.

Vegetarians and carnivores alike loved Ocean Benson's recipes and drove to the exurbs and negotiated his fishing-road of a driveway in any weather to buy what he cooked.

Ocean Benson was an ovo-lacto vegetarian. Meaning that dairy products and eggs were permitted in his diet. In the harsh winter months when nothing grew, he took commercial advantage of his diet by experimenting with recipes.

Out of his house and his kitchen, Ocean sold vegetarian dishes, as many as possible cooked from produce he grew, then canned, dried and stored in his root cellar.

A favorite:

OCEAN'S MEATLESSLOAF

Time of preparation: Two hours.

Ingredients: 5 ½ cups of water, 2 cups long-grain brown rice, 1 cup lentils, 2 cups Italian sauce, 1 cup minced garlic, 1 pound shredded cheddar cheese.

Steps:

1. In a large pot, bring the water to a boil.
2. Stir in the rice and lentils.
3. Cover and simmer for 45 minutes or until the liquid is absorbed.
4. With a large spoon or fork, combine the Italian sauce, garlic and cheddar until completely incorporated. *
5. Pour the mixture into 2 loaf pans (preferably glass) that have been coated with cooking oil spray.
6. Bake at 350° for 45 minutes.
7. It pairs nicely with a California zinfandel.

* Ocean had made over 50 Meatlessloaf recipes, each one a bit different; He likened them to snowflakes. Instead of Italian sauce, perhaps use salsa or vindaloo. Also, add wilted spinach, oatmeal, caramelized onions, hot sauce, shredded carrots, *ad infinitum*. A Meatlessloaf is an excellent instrument for cleaning out the fridge.

A newspaper food reporter, recipient of word-of-mouth, came by, interviewed Ocean and took some pictures. A few days later in his column, he wrote that *Ocean Benson's Meatlessloaf was so good that it should not be so good for you. Ocean's Meatlessloaf defies The Law of Culinary Unfairness.*

On this Wednesday, December 7, 2005, Ocean sold out of Ocean's Meatlessloaf in less than an hour. Inside, cleaning up, he thought of the quarrel he and Quyen had in the morning, a rare occurrence, even when they were infants.

It happened in the kitchen while they were making

Ocean's Meatlessloaf.

Ocean saw something unseen in Quyen, and asked her if she was happy.

She said she was happy.

Not 100% happy, he said.

He'd seen this in her recently; something unseen on the surface, hidden from everybody but him.

Who is that happy, she rebutted? Ninety percent of the time, okay?

He said, okay, more like 50%.

They went back and forth, as if bargaining on a used car.

They settled for 65%, upon which she left without a good-bye.

He continued cleaning up, missing her already.

Her storming out will be a first-run feature in his nightmares for some time.

* The Law of Culinary Unfairness states that foods like bacon that taste good are bad for you and foods like watercress that don't taste good are good for you.

≈≈≈

Speaking of used cars, a neighbor of Brenda Wilson got David Wilson a job selling used cars. Brenda was anything but senile. She'd had a bellyful of David lounging around the house, sneaking booze, as if she couldn't tell.

My way or the highway, she'd said.

A chastened David nodded. It'd be her way.

David Wilson's sales manager was an in-your-face born-again Christian, alcoholic and a crook.

David was a lot of things, but he was not a crook. He quit in disgust before making a sale and went across the street to work for a competitor.

His new sales manager was a boozer too and a skirt chaser who liked to play the ponies, but he was not a religious hypocrite and he was not a crook.

David made his first sale, on a late-model Acura RL, taking a seven-year-old Honda Accord LX as a trade-in.

He treated the customer fairly, as did his sales manager.

David Wilson earned a $275 commission. It was a far cry from his day-trading heyday, but it felt good.

Damn good.

David Wilson had found his calling.

≈≈≈

U-2003 and its long-dead occupants had not budged from Sudoeste Isla Island. Seven countries were fighting over it and them.

A tent city sprang up and the island's population soared to 224.

So intense was the squabble nobody noticed that the three Paraguayan passports vanished.

WAXWING, CEDAR A. *May 13, 2006 promised to be a mild, dry Saturday. It was a fine morning to go birding. With the financial help of Jim and Laura Wilson, Brenda Wilson and Gwen Carter, both 81, were able to live in apartments in an upscale senior community complex. It offered recreational facilities, good meals (should a resident choose not to cook or be unable to), and field trips such as the one Brenda and Gwen were on.*

Brenda had become an avid birder who talked and talked about the killdeer family that had nested in their backyard. How Dave let the grass grow. The new friends they made in the neighborhood. How they'd loved her cookies.

The community's small bus transported Brenda and Gwen, nine other residents, and their leader, an expert birder who volunteered for this and other senior communities. He was in the first crop of baby boomers.

A child at age 60, they teased.

They arrived at their destination, a wildlife refuge. It was a low marshy area with a boardwalk that was easy going for the seniors.

The leader saw and heard them before his group. Pausing and setting his scope, he directed his people where to aim their binoculars and said they were welcome to look through his scope too.

All were excited. They were seeing a wealth of birds. Chickadees, herons, warblers, jays, wrens, sparrows, blackbirds, finches, grosbeaks, siskins, and a variety of waterfowl.

The birding expert was really excited when he spotted a cedar waxwing. Its wings were grayish, with a small slash of red feathers. It had a light tan body and a woodpecker's profile, black feathers around the eyes and the top of its beak.

It was on a twig, as if posing for them.

Cedar waxwings had a large habitat, the leader whispered, but were rare at this refuge.

Brenda Wilson focused her binoculars on the beautiful bird. She was excited too.

The cedar waxwing was the last thing she ever saw.

≈≈≈

Jim Wilson and Laura Wilson were notified first by Brenda Wilson's senior home.

They were updating the blog Laura had set up for their charitable foundation, a foundation they decided to leave unnamed, as vanity had no place in what they hoped to do.

≈≈≈

Jim Wilson notified his younger brothers, Richard Wilson first.

Richard Wilson, Ophelia, Wilson and 10-year-old Richard Junior were at the zoo. They were at that moment looking through glass, watching penguins swim underwater.

Young Richard was a quiet and polite lad, a chip off the old block of his father/uncle and/or uncle/father.

≈≈≈

When Jim notified David Junior, he was in the main bathroom of his childhood home he was buying from his mother. He had been cinching his tie, on his way in to work. He had taken over as sales manager at the dealership when his predecessor was hospitalized for cirrhosis of the liver.

They ran a full page ad in the morning paper. David was expecting a big turnout today.

≈≈≈

When Laura notified their daughter, Dr. Quyen Wilson, she was studying an X-ray of a healing femur, bored to tears.

The tears that immediately followed were not tears of boredom.

WINGNUT. *A word with multiple definitions, some proper, some slang.*

On Tuesday, July 4, 2006, the 30th anniversary of Elmer Free Carter's death, Gwen Carter chose a shoebox at eye level in one of four columns which were neatly stacked against a wall in her senior-community apartment. She did so out of habit and to get her mind off her dear friend, Brenda Wilson.

She brought it out carefully and took it to her desk. The 13AAA gym-shoe box was the biggest of all. Gwen imagined it belonging to a football or basketball player. Gwen could use those sneakers as water skis.

This biggest box had the smallest contents she had yet seen — one sheet of paper from a half-sized notepad. The sheet of paper was upside down, taped to the bottom of the box.

She pulled it off, turned it over, and read: *How many different meanings does WINGNUT have?*

Gwen thought a wingnut was a tightener on a bolt that you twist with your thumb and index finger.

Period.

She opened the lid of her laptop computer and turned it on. The machines were getting smaller and cheaper all the time. The technology was incredible, she thought, right out of Buck Rogers.

Gwen unplugged her telephone cord from the wall and plugged her computer cord into it.

When the computer warmed up, Gwen clicked on her Internet page and typed in her password.

When it came up a minute later, she clicked on what they called a search engine.

She typed *Wingnut definition.*

A page appeared on her screen. It had a dozen definitions for wingnut, everything from the hardware part she knew to a crazy person to a fan of the Detroit Red Wings hockey team. She printed the page and shut down the computer.

She looked at the printed page and her father's note for the longest time.

The answer jumped off the page at her.

She heard her father's voice saying that *if you think there's a pat solution for everything you're a goddamn fool.*

X-RAY VISION NEVERMORE. *August 2, 2007. It was predicted to be the hottest day of the year, at 101° a record temperature for that date.*

This was the date of the grand opening of the offices of Dr. Quyen Wilson, General Practitioner.

Her clinic was on Main Street of a small town near Ocean's organic farm, which he had formally renamed Benson Organic Farm, LLC.

The small town, like many small American towns, was not prosperous. It had been desiccated by sterile suburban malls and big box stores. If you ignored the vacant storefronts, the town was picturesque, with angled parking, and old brick and wooden buildings.

The town was in a 1950s time warp.

Dr. Wilson's clinic was air-conditioned, the system already on full throttle in the early morning. She was holding a reception in the lobby, starting at 10 a.m.

Come on by. Meet the doctor and help yourself to soda, iced tea, pastries and hors d'oeuvres.

His insistent suggestion and the percentage negotiations of almost two years ago?

Quyen thought that Ocean Benson was nudging her out of his life. A girlfriend on the side? She was pushing 40 and learning to deeply resent him.

Not so. He was nudging her into working increased

hours at the radiology lab, consulting on the most difficult cases. Ocean was demanding that Dr. Wilson do what she hated to do for a reason. He wanted her to save money to do what she was going to start doing this morning after the reception.

She needed seed money and then some, money for this office and equipment and to support her in the long haul until her appointment book filled up.

Even then, Quyen's income promised to be iffy.

Her practice was to be exclusively for those without medical insurance.

They will be charged what they can afford to pay.

If she had to, to make ends meet, she'd work one day a week as a radiologist.

Dr. Wilson couldn't wait for the ten o'clock, to do what she dreamt of doing.

She loved Ocean even more.

And told him so as he put the finishing touches on the vegetarian hors d'oeuvres supplied by Benson Organic Farm, LLC.

Y

Y, THE LETTER, IS NOT IN ONE OF THE LONGEST WORDS IN THE ENGLISH LANGUAGE – ANTIDISESTABLISHMENTARIANISM. *Twenty-eight letters, but no "Y".*

That factoid roamed through Laura Wilson's mind on September 9, 2009 as she surfed for charities worthy of a $10,000 savings bond in their unnamed foundation. Twenty-six letters in the alphabet, 28 letters in the humungous word, a surplus of two. Yet "Y" was an orphan.

The probability of that? She'd have to have pen and paper. The odds might be surprisingly long.

Casinos made a bundle on keno, a few dollars at a time. A game with surprisingly long odds, a deceptively difficult game to win.

She had been fiddling with numerical anomalies and patterns and palindromes: 0-1-2-3-2-1-0. If a date, it'd be 012/32/10, or December 32, 2010.

Silly.

Today's date wasn't so silly. Wednesday September 9, 2009. Or 09/09/09.

Insert 9:09 o'clock. Nine minutes after nine on September 9, 2009. Is 09:09/09/09/09.

Consecutive numbers too: 2-3-4-5-6-7. Is 2:03:04 on May 6, 2007.

Surfing and games, as she ate a sandwich.

To Laura, the equivalent of bread and circuses.

YUCATÁN MEXICO, CAMPECHE CITY. *April 8, 2010. Two men met in a bar in a rough neighborhood in this grand old walled city on the Yucatán peninsula's west coast. The bar had swinging doors as if in a Western movie and a portable TV over the bar tuned to soccer games and boxing.*

Young locals who made it a tough neighborhood were wary of two gringos who sat a table, and stayed out of their way. They knew tough when they saw it.

The short, stocky guy with the cigar and the gold chains introduced himself to the other guy as Big Vinnie.

The other guy was wearing a guayubera and dark sunglasses. He shook Big Vinnie's hand. He offered no name.

Guy in the shades, whoever the fuck he was, he looked to Big Vinnie like some sort of A-rab or spic-jig combo.

Looked like one of them fanatic fuckers who blow up airliners.

Big Vinnie started it off by taking from his shirt pocket a coin sealed in plastic and cardboard saying: See, on the obverse side, coin talk for heads, the old boy with the fancy jacket. On the reverse (turning it over), it says in the Mexican language The Mexican United States One Peso.

Big Vinnie said he'd translated it outta a two-language dictionary book.

See the date, 1963? Now (turning over the coin), see on the old boy, who was a revolutionist from the old days named (takes a slip of paper out of his pocket) Jose Morelos y Pavon. A mouthful, ain't it?

You see fingerprint powder and a fingerprint you can make out easy, which (taking a folded slip of paper out of a back pocket that he unfolded) matches up exact with the thumb print on this here booking slip the Dallas Police Department made on November 22, 1963 after they went and arrested the schmo who shot JFK and later on in the same day whacked out a Dallas cop named J. D. Tippit who'd stopped him on the street.

Big Vinnie said he wasn't saying how this coin had come into his possession, but the history of it is that this Lee Harvey Oswald, he went to Mexico City like in late September before he clipped JFK to see if he could get one of them visas to go to Cuba.

He went to the Soviet Union Russia and Cuba embassies down there to get this done. The embassies, both of them, right off they saw Oswald as a nut job. They bounced him back and forth, fucking with him till he gave up and came back to Dallas and did what he did.

After he did it and it was all over the news, the maid in the hotel room Oswald stayed at in Mexico City saw the news and went through Oswald's room with a fine-toothed comb and found this here peso coin hid someplace like under his mattress that he forgot about when he packed to go on account of he was so pissed off that they wouldn't let him go to Cuba to be with that cigar-smoking Commie he thought was such a hot shit.

So there it is, pal. Let's see what you got.

The man in the guayubera wearing dark glasses was not an Arab. He did not blow up airliners. The man had a variety of business interests, buying and selling and trading.

He looked at the coin and the booking sheet. He looked at this Big Vinnie too, his stupid nickname proof that he was a wise guy. This shrimp with the cigar and gold chains.

Little Big Vinnie.

He took an envelope from a soft briefcase and gave it to *Little* Big Vinnie.

In the envelope were three Paraguayan passports.

Big Vinnie opened them and said, it is okay, even-steven, mine for yours?

No, not quite. Your coin is ancient history and its provenance is questionable. My part of the transaction is big news.

Provenance? Big Vinnie wondered what the fuck his peso had to do with some Rhode Island city. He told the guy that, yeah, the passports are big news. This makes them hotter'n a popcorn fart. No way can you move them now. We'd be sitting on them for who knows how long. Our dough treading water, you know.

Big Vinnie offered to throw in some cash.

The man in the guayubera said it wasn't enough.

Vinnie said him and his boys collected other things.

Like the world's first products. The world's first box of them zipper-lock things you store leftovers in. The world's first non-stick fry pan. The first pack of them yellow stickum notes.

Hang on to 'em, sell 'em to museums later on.

The man in the guayubera politely declined.

They bargained and came to an agreement.

Little Big Vinnie peeled bills from a roll and fanned them out on the table.

They went their separate ways without a handshake, but with what each wanted.

≈≈≈

Laura Wilson was besieged with requests. Word of her charity spread fast. The Internet was like millions of old ladies gossiping over the fence, she thought.

Electronic old ladies gossiping over the Ethernet fence.

Among the charities Jim and Laura checked out online was *Art in its Rightful Place*, a foundation with the stated goal of seeking out art and collectables connected to important historical events that had been stolen or otherwise turned up in the wrong hands, and return them to the "rightfful" owners.

If the "rightfful" owners couldn't be located, they'd sell the collectibles and donate the "proseeds" to charity.

The Wilsons were unable to penetrate past the home page of their website, which had more misspellings.

No names were given for its officers.

Jim and Laura concluded that it was an amateurish hustle at best.

At the worst, a front for a criminal organization dealing in stolen items of historical interest.

Art in its Rightfful Place's request for a $10,000 United States Savings Bond was denied.

Z

ZULU IS FOR "Z", THE 26TH AND LAST LETTER IN THE PHONETIC ALPHABET.

December 21, 2012 – the end of the 5125-year-long cycle in the Mayan Long Count Calendar.

This is the end of our tall tale too.

Controversial and inaccurate as all end-of-the-world prophesies have been (just ask the Jehovah's Witnesses), scholars disagree if that date is a prediction at all, or if there were different Maya calendars with different doomsdays.

Pinning down the end of the world is tricky business.

If, however, you are reading this novel after December 21, 2012, an apocalypse did not occur.

If, however, you are not reading this novel after December 21, 2012, either the apocalypse did occur –

– you started reading A BOOK OF FACTS and stopped, putting it aside and muttering "what a piece of shit".

– you chose not to read it at all.

Regardless, herewith, therefore, the surviving cast of characters and what's going on in their lives:

Benson, Mary Ann (1930-). Lives on the same floor as Gwen Carter at the upscale senior community complex. Has her eye on a grocery bagger at a supermarket two blocks away. He's a sweet boy with thick wrists and a nice ass. If he'll go out with an octogenarian lady, he has kinky tastes. That's a given. She'll he happy to paddle his gorgeous little butt with her cane. All he needs to do is ask.

Wilson-Benson, Dr. Quyen (1968-). Is going into labor with their first child. She'll be 44 on June 10, ± five days, so their daughter will be an only child.

Benson, Ocean (1970-). Is with her in the delivery room.

Carter, Gwen (1924-). Has most of her meals prepared and brought to her room. Not because she's frail. She's going through Elmer Free Benson's shoeboxes and wants to peruse them all while she still can. She's reading 14 single-spaced pages on how to unscramble eggs. It's actually making sense. When done reading, she's going downstairs to the kitchen for a dozen.

Wilson, David Junior (1955-). Is dry and sober. He's overall sales manager at the dealership where he broke into the business and five other dealerships owned by the same corporation. Never married, David is in a serious relationship with a divorced woman with three kids who bought a new minivan from one of the dealerships.

Wilson, Kellı° (1963-). Has been married and divorced four times. Kellı° has put on a little weight and dresses too tightly. Kelli° and her cottage-cheese thighs is a walking-talking, living-breathing muffin top.

Wilson, Ophelia (1953-). Ran off with a quadruplet and divorced Richard.

Wilson, Richard (1955-). Is a full-time employee and manager of Benson Organic Farm, LLC. The farm has expanded, purchasing 100 acres of adjacent property.

Wilson, Richard Junior (1996-). High-school student

and part-time employee of Benson Organic Farm, LLC, works there after school and on weekends.

Wilson, Jim (1946-) and Laura Wilson (1945-). In mid-2011, a French probe passed Venus, to slingshot itself around the sun, to increase velocity for a long journey. As it passed Venus, it picked up a weak signal on the same frequency as a Chinese probe believed to have been lost in 2003. The probe's high-resolution camera was gimbaled. Mission directors turned it toward the source of the signal and were astounded by what they saw.

A planetarium in financial trouble accepted five $10,000 United States Savings Bonds from Jim and Laura Wilson's unnamed foundation in exchange for naming it The James Wilson Planetarium.

With a bottle of champagne, the Wilsons are celebrating two things.

A woman who had worked for Laura on the Y2K team phoned to wish her a Happy New Year and to apologize for forgetting the West Indies vacation and the newspaper on the palapa bar. She told Laura of the Bob Jones obit. Laura and the woman thought it was a long shot, Bob Jones a common name, but Laura accepted it as Father Sir and celebrated his demise.

They are celebrating with a capital "C" the front-page story on the discovery of two Venusian moons, crediting the Aphrodite and Gerund discoveries to Mr. James Wilson.

Thirty-four planetariums have so far emailed him congratulations.

They are celebrating in and on the back seat of their 1962 Chevrolet Impala convertible.

By Laura's calculation, it is the 17,243rd day since their first romp on the Naugahyde.

Total number of romps — incalculable.

The End (Almost)

If you stop being silly, it's all over.

— Anonymous

The End

Thank you for reading.
Please review this book. Reviews help others find Absolutely Amazing eBooks and inspire us to keep providing these marvelous tales.

If you would like to be put on our email list to receive updates on new releases, contests, and promotions, please go to AbsolutelyAmazingEbooks.com and sign up.

About the Author

Gary Alexander has written 16 novels, including *Loot,* fourth in the mystery series featuring comic Buster Hightower. *Disappeared*, the first in the series, has been optioned to Universal Studios. And *Dragon Lady*, his Vietnam novel, was recently published.

He's written 150+ short stories and sold travel articles to 6 major dailies. One story appeared in *Best American Mystery Stories 2010*, another in *Ice Cold*, last year's Mystery Writers of America anthology.

Alexander is a nonsmoking, nondrinking vegetarian. He does, however, abuse caffeine and chocolate.

His website is www.garyralexander.com.

The New Atlantian Library

New AtlantianLibrary.com
or AbsolutelyAmazingEbooks.com
or AA-eBooks.com

www.ingramcontent.com/pod-product-compliance
Lightning Source LLC
LaVergne TN
LVHW020540100826
845148LV00010B/1543
9780692438602